CW01219038

BRISTLE

Copyright © 2015 Chris Boothman.
All rights reserved.
First paperback edition printed 2015

No part of this book shall be reproduced or transmitted in any form or by any means,
electronic or mechanical, including photocopying, recording, or by any information retrieval
system without written permission of the publisher.

Published by RWBA Publishing Ltd
Tel: 0843 636 5956
Designed and Set by RWBA Publishing Ltd
Tel: 0843 636 5956

RWBA PUBLISHING LTD

For more copies of this book, please email: sales@rwba.co.uk or via through Amazon

Printed by CreateSpace

<u>Acknowledgement and Disclaimer</u>
This book contains a number of stories from my life and those of my friends and family. There are also some that are completely fictional. I would like to thank everyone for letting me use those stories. None of the characters in this book relate to any individual alive or dead.

Although every precaution has been taken in the preparation of this book, the publisher and
author assume no responsibility for errors or omissions. Neither is any liability assumed for
damages resulting from the use of this information contained herein.

BRISTLE

By Chris Boothman

Bristle

Foreword

This book is unequal parts biography, autobiography and fiction. I've long watched others and myself relate stories of youth during lock-ins and on lads nights out and finally got round to putting some of these together woven among a series coming of age accounts that I have based in Bristol.

I moved to Bristol as a late teenager and found it to be a marvellous city which excited this country-boy and welcomed him into its heart with the typical generosity of the wonderful people I met there. Its eclectic mix of the criminal, working, middle and upper classes make it vibrant and bohemian and full of opportunities to all the dreamers that exist there. I have tried in some part to convey that but have almost definitely failed as there is only one way to enjoy such treasures ... in person.

A word of warning: The story revolves around four lads in their late teens who, as is the nature of such things, use colourful language and encounter colourful situations. I am someone who abhors swearing in public but understands that life must be a case of each to his own. For realism I have tried to reflect that language and describe in sufficient detail those situations that they faced. This means that you will definitely find some extreme language and extreme scenes.

If there is any chance that you could be offended by such matters I urge you to read no further.

Chris Boothman
Author

The Story so far

Jimmy leant back against the stained velour seat with one hand resting on the gear stick and the other caressing the leatherette steering wheel cover (with plastic walnut burr effect inserts) idly watching the pink furry 'cock and balls' hanging from the rear view mirror, sway evocatively from side to side. A smile crept across his lips as he remembered the day his sister, Vickie, gave them to him. He knew it was a joke and she couldn't stop chuckling as she handed over the hastily wrapped present on his birthday (Christmas trees and robins in mid-July) and as inappropriate as it was, Jimmy took it as positively as always. "It's so other cars know you're a DICK!" she spat before giggling. For all their arguments and fights growing up, he was clearly always in her thoughts. The rest of the lads weren't too impressed and didn't exactly see the funny side. In truth he could see their point of view. The car was a joint project and all decisions on it were made democratically. If it hadn't been for Symon's outburst (he'd had a bad day), the hour long project meeting over the suitability of the 'cock and balls' motif might have raged on into the night. "Oh for fuck's sake who gives a shit! Let 'em hang there forever or throw them in the bin!" he shouted. After a brief period of furtive looks at each other and one or two mouthed "Oooh get him!" the conversation had moved on.

Jimmy's reverie was broken by the windscreen wipers swishing across the window. They weren't on *intermittent*, they were on *broken* and regardless of the position of the switch, they and only they chose when it was necessary to move. The windscreen had misted up so Jimmy reached for the glove compartment which like a himitsu-bako puzzle box required a specific list of actions to be performed in a set order before it would open and reveal its valuable contents. In this case the gentle press on the top left corner followed by lifting the clasp, a tap to the bottom middle and a hard bang to the dash above revealed a box of tissues, some fuses, a couple of bulbs (one dead, one working), a large packet of condoms (unopened), a small tin of 'tobacco', some Rizlas and a sponge.

As he leant forward to wipe the window clear of condensation, a loud bang shook the car as a body landed on the bonnet and a face slid forward pressing grotesquely against the windscreen. Unimpassionately Jimmy looked at the gurning face of Sid and continued wiping the windscreen. Sid rolled off the bonnet and hopped into the back seat. "Wankah!" he grunted in greeting. "Spankah!" Jimmy replied. It was their way.
Sid reached forward and banged the dash above the centre console. The radio sparked into life and the velvet tones of DJ Ed Swarthy poured into the car. "Oh I hate this

twat!" Sid grunted. "He's such a knob jockey!" Jimmy smiled. "It's a pre-requisite of the job. On the application form it doesn't ask IF you are a knob jockey – it asks how MUCH of a knob jockey you are! On his application form he put five stars then scribbled it out and drew five knobs with hairy balls and man juice spurting out of them." Sid chuckled. Everybody likes the agreement of others. "Yeah! He also took out some aftershave and sprayed the form with it and drew a big kiss in the top right corner with his lipstick! And then he reached inside his pants and ..." This was too much for Jimmy. "Alright, alright! TMI mate! You've always got to take it that extra mile!" Sid threw himself back into the seat giggling at what he would have said.

DJ Ed Swarthy finished his sentence as the next track eased its way gently between his words. Sid began to idly drum the beat on the back of Jimmy's seat. The tinny synth crackled through the speakers before the slightly warbling voice of Madonna pushed the tune into the background. As the song rambled on aimlessly the car began to rock gently from side to side. Jimmy looked into the rear-view mirror to symbolically question Sid. He shrugged and joined Jimmy in looking around. The rocking steadily increased until Sid and Jimmy had to grip their seats. A loud banging cacophony echoed from strong slaps on the roof before the passenger side front and rear doors opened and Symon and Sean bundled inside. "Wankahs!" they chorused. "Spankahs!" Jimmy and Sid replied. It was their way. Bless. Madonna faded out as DJ Ed Swarthy introduced the next track in his 'Tribute to the 80s' playlist. The synthetic drum beat edged up slowly in volume as DJ Ed Swarthy faded out. The syrupy and powerful voice of Annie Lennox silenced the four lads. Eventually Sean chimed in. "She's right. Sweet dreams ARE made of this. Mates together having a laugh." Symon nodded. "Wankahs and spankahs together." They all burst into laughter.

As Sean asked Symon how training went, Jimmy drifted away from the conversation into a dreamy memory of the first time the four of them had met. It was a warm morning and Jimmy was stood leaning against the wall outside of the metalwork shop at Southmead Community College waiting for the teacher Mr Graeme "hey man" Stewartson to turn up. Jimmy heard the scuffing of trainers and the twang of a bouncing ball from around the corner. He turned to look as a lithe lad in a tracksuit glided along with the ball seemingly attached to his feet. He stepped over it, flicked it over his head, bent forward and caught it in the crook of his neck. He opened the sports bag he was carrying and let the ball roll down his arm and into it. He threw his bag next to Jimmy and sat on it leaning against the wall. Not even the slightest out of breath he looked up at Jimmy and stated "Thought I was gonna be late! Had early morning practice." Symon went on to introduce himself and explain that he was an apprentice at Bristol Rovers Football Club and had been put on this college course as part of his deal. Jimmy wasn't into football much and his family were City supporters but it was still interesting to chat to someone who played sport for money. Next round the corner was Sean. He was dressed head to foot in camouflage gear and the faint whiff of earth suffused with gun oil followed him. "Hey." he said simply as he sat on the grass facing Jimmy and Symon.

Symon feigned surprise saying "Sorry, didn't see you there!" as a wry smile sneaked across his face. Sean looked himself up and down and chuckled. "Been shooting with Dad. Well walking mostly. Didn't see anything to shoot." Jimmy nodded in understanding. Sean lived on the outskirts of the City though his parents farm was steadily being swallowed up by the seemingly endless encroachment of the rapidly expanding city. Finally Sid ambled across the grass and flopped down next to Sean. "Why does this place have to be so far from the road?" Jimmy smiled at his lifelong friend. "Cos they know you need the exercise bud!" Sid was a little

Bristle

overweight but so far in his life he had been OK with it. Sean felt an itch creeping up his thigh and reached inside his trousers to scratch it. Quick as a flash Symon shouted "Wankah!" and slapped his hand away. Sean looked aghast. Symon explained that in the academy, anyone caught scratching their balls on the pitch got slapped. He said "It's like our version of slapping someone's bum." Still shocked, Sean mumbled "Bunch of spankers if you ask me!" A pause ensued followed by a chuckle breaking out among all four of them. "That's us," said Jimmy, "Wankahs and Spankahs!"

DJ Ed Swarthy talked over the last few bars of Annie, informing all who listened that the news was coming after the next track – a classic from Dire Straits with their 'Walk of life'. The four lads gently boogied away in their seats to the iconic Knopfler guitar riff.
"So what's the sitch with the motor Jimmer?" Sean asked quietly. "Well we've nearly got enough to do the tyres which will mean we can get it off the blocks but I think we should wait till everything else is done before we do that. The engine needs some work and I'll do that this weekend if we buy a new carburettor." Symon nodded. "How much?" Jimmy grimaced. "Should be £150 if we buy new but I reckon I could get one from a scrapper for maybe £20?" The rest of the lads looked at each other before reaching into

their pockets and handing three fivers to Jimmy. "I'll go and look Saturday morning and see what I can find. What are you up to Slymes?" Symon looked up from staring at his feet. "Got a game Saturday afternoon at Swindon. Meeting at the ground 10ish then coach ride down the M4. Should be back for 6." Jimmy turned to the back seat. "What about you two?" Sean spoke first. "Farm stuff in the morning then nothing." Sid added, "Food shopping with Mum in the morning then off to watch the rugby in the afternoon. Be back for 6ish." Jimmy picked up a cloth from the door pocket and started polishing the steering wheel. "So we all set to meet here about 7 then down the boozer?" Everyone nodded.

One by one Symon, Sean and Sid said their goodbyes and got out of the car leaving Jimmy polishing the dash. Eventually he turned the ignition off and scrambled out of the driver's seat. Making sure not to step on the wire leading from the constantly hooked up battery charger that ran into the house through a slightly open window, Jimmy walked towards his house. Standing on the steps he looked back at their pride and joy and briefly longed for the day when they could take it off the bricks and actually go somewhere. It had been two years since they clubbed together and bought it from the scrap yard and many hours of work had gone into getting it to this stage. A deep sigh preceded Jimmy opening the front door and walking inside.

As Jimmy walked to the kitchen he popped his head round the living room door and asked "Cuppa anyone?" Sat on the fading DFS sofa his Mum looked up and smiled "Yes please luvver." His Dad added, "And fer me son." Jimmy continued into the kitchen, flicked on the light and grabbed the kettle. Filling it at the sink he gazed lovingly out of the window at his car. The water began to flow out of the kettle till Jimmy realised when he turned off the tap and put the lid on it. He slotted it onto its base and flicked the switch. The blue glow of the clear plastic switch reflected off the shiny counter. Jimmy reached into the cupboard above and got out three cups. He dropped a tea bag in each, two sugars in his and his Dad's and a sweetener in his Mum's. Opening the fridge he pulled out the bottle of milk, removed the cap and sniffed. "That'll do." He mused. He poured a little over an inch of milk into each cup and heard the kettle click as he put the bottle back into the fridge. Pouring the steaming water into each cup as he stirred, subconsciously evaluating the colour, he mentally checked off each cup as he went. He put the kettle back onto its base before using the spoon to squeeze each tea bag against the side of the cup and drop it on a plate next to the box of tea bags. The tea bag plate made no sense to Jimmy. Nobody ever took a tea bag from the plate and reused it. It was, to all intents and purposes, simply a stopping off point for tea bags. It was an assembly point midway between the sink and the bin where they all ultimately arrived but after a useless couple of days wait at tea-bag plate central. Grabbing all three cups carefully by their handles in one hand he walked out of the kitchen and into the lounge. He put one next to his Mum and one by his Dad before slumping into the spare chair and focusing on whatever they had on the television. "You're joking?" he sighed. "Not this again!" His Dad looked over and said "Shut it! This is a classic! They don't make TV like this no more." Jimmy sighed again. "There's a reason for that Dad – it's crap!" Jimmy's mother looked across at him in shock. "Ere, Prince of pooh! There's no better characters than Del and Rodders! They's real people! None of yer skiffy crap ere!" Jimmy slowly shook his head and got up. "It's Sci-Fi Mum!"

In despair he left the lounge and climbed the stairs. He stopped in the toilet for a quick wee before throwing himself on his bed. He reached for his laptop, opened the screen and logged in to RW3DCHAT and began moving his avatar around the mystical 3D world. He saw little going on so decided to teleport to his favourite spot in the enchanted forest next to a multi-colour waterfall called 'The Tears of Tersis' that he could hide behind and watch the world go by, not that much of this virtual world was going anywhere as it wasn't until the Americans logged in later that the place got really busy.

After a long day working with Paul, his boss, his eyelids soon felt heavy and leaning on his arm he drifted off to sleep. He awoke with a start an hour later to the sound of insistent pings coming from his laptop. As his eyes focused he saw message after message from 'Princess Alicia' wondering where he was and why he wasn't answering. He quickly typed an apology and reason as her avatar materialised next to him under the waterfall. Her character stood there with arms open wide awaiting a hug so he pressed F5 and his character stood and hugged her back. They both sat down on the stone ledge and looked through the myriad changing colours of the cascading water in front of them. "So how was work Studly?" Her message popped up onto his screen. "Oh not bad Princess. Paul drove us up to a 'mall' in Cheltenham to replace a couple of store front windows and put up some new advertising film on a couple of others. He's well happy that he got into the advertising stuff. Those films are dead easy to have made up and with a bit of common sense and washing up liquid they go onto the glass easy as pie." A 'LOL' reply appeared almost immediately. "I love your sayings Studly. Easy as pie!" Jimmy and Princess Alicia talked for over an hour before they said their goodbyes. Within seconds of closing his laptop and still fully dressed, Jimmy passed into the land of sleep not stirring until the sunlight shone through his window the next morning.

Like an old man, Jimmy eased himself out of bed and tried to stretch the discomfort of sleeping in one position out of his aching back. Zombielike and eyes still partially shut, Jimmy stumbled into the bathroom. He was halfway through brushing his teeth while standing over the toilet praying for his 'morning wood' to go down enough to pee before he noticed the sound of the shower. Vickie, eyes closed tight and stinging from some errant shampoo, fumbled for the shower button and switched it off. She turned and stumbled out of the cubicle with her hands desperately searching for the towel rack and relief from her painful eyes. Unfortunately she was totally disoriented and rather than feeling the soft fluffy texture of the towels, she felt the slightly clammy and hard touch of a shoulder. Confused she explored further with her hands until she realised the shape of a human body. Her scream surprised them both. She opened her eyes and stared at her brother until the pain forced her to close them again. Jimmy jumped slightly at the shriek and, as often happens in moments of shock, his muscles relaxed. His previously torpid tumescence wilted under the heat of the moment and that which had previously been blocked issued forth with gusto just as his relaxing jaw released its grip on his toothbrush and allowed it to cartwheel through the golden stream into the waiting toilet bowl. Vickie turned and ran, grabbing a towel as she went, leaving Jimmy staring slack-jawed at the bright crimson bouncing cheeks of his sisters' rapid retreat. He finally awoke and flushed the toilet. Happy to see his toothbrush had remained, he reached in and grabbed it, rinsed it briefly in the sink and then took it with him into the shower where he finished brushing his teeth under the warm trickle of the last of the hot water.

A Night Out

Jimmy sat quietly in the passenger seat of the van as Paul drove them back from Cheltenham. The job of apprentice to Paul was one which Jimmy enjoyed but not because of the work, it was hardly taxing, nor the variety but entirely because of Paul. Jimmy had grown up knowing only those in his family and community. He had not had exposure to others from different backgrounds and in truth had developed, or more fairly inherited, a certain prejudice against the middle and upper classes. But Paul had quickly and easily washed away that bigotry with his quiet, calm and confident air. He was a straight shooter and could always be relied upon for an honest opinion.

Jimmy realised from day one working with Paul that he could trust him, principally because Paul took him as he found him and expected others to do the same. When talking with customers he was always polite but never subservient. There was so much of the role model in Paul that Jimmy had not found at home. His father was a good man but was more a friend than a father. As a child, Jimmy had come to realise, a boy particularly needed a father more than a friend. But his Dad had become a father through circumstance not planning. In some of his kinder reflective moods Jimmy realised that his Dad has always done his best and that it was probably always easier to be a father figure when doing so part time. Paul only had to deal with him 40 hours a week whereas his father had to do so 24/7. Even the best of friends would fall out when spending so much time together.

"So what are your plans for the rest of the weekend? Sorry again that I had to bring you in on this emergency job on a Saturday morning Jimmy." Paul said. "Oh no worries. I was going to go to the scrap yard and get a carb for the car but I can do that tomorrow." Jimmy replied jovially. "Oh no Jimmy! I'm so sorry! Look, let's go there now. It's been ages since I've had a good rummage round a scrap yard and it will save you getting a lift there and back if I take you." After a short period of rebuffed objections Jimmy succumbed and Paul took the road toward the scrap yard rather than the usual one back to Jimmy's house. When they arrived, they owner of the car parts shop come scrap yard scowled at them as he was just about to shut early but Paul slipped him a fiver and said "Just give us half an hour please. We're here to spend not just look about." Jimmy knew exactly where the yard's stock of his car were stacked and lead Paul straight there. It reminded Paul of the assault courses he spent so much time on during his time in the army before that fateful day when he turned his ankle and snapped his Achilles while out on manoeuvres. It spelt the end of his army career and probably saved his life as his unit was only a fortnight away from deployment. But those thoughts quickly evaporated as Paul breathed in the unique smell of the scrap yard. Old oil, petrol, earth and decay all mingled together to form a perfume every ounce capable of strong Madeleine moments. Paul had lagged behind a little but following the noise found Jimmy half under the bonnet of the bottom rust bucket in a pile of four. Reaching into his back pocket, Jimmy retrieved a spanner and deftly undid a few bolts covering the carburettor. The odd expletive followed before Jimmy slid out from under the bonnet. "What's up Pal?" Paul asked. "That one's knackered. I'd checked the others out before and this was my last hope. That's the problem with scrappers, water and rust." Paul sighed. "That sucks mate. Is there anything else you need while we're here?" Jimmy shook his head. "I've got some serious electrical problems and I think it may need replacing the entire wiring loom. I've looked at each individual device that's playing up and they seem fine. It's a bullet I don't wanna bite." Paul nodded. "Well if you're done here how about I take you for a quick pint at the pub to console you?" Jimmy nodded though couldn't smile through his disappointment in not finding a working carburettor. Just as they reached the van, Paul shouted back to

Bristle

the man as he was closing the gate to stop and rushed over to him. He spoke to him for a couple of seconds, patted his pockets then fished out his keys and turned back to Jimmy. "Thought I'd dropped my keys in there!" he said apologetically. They hopped in the van and set off for the pub.

The "couple of drinks" had turned into five or six with Paul not letting Jimmy buy a single round. When Jimmy finally got home he was fit for little more than sitting in front of the TV and snoozing for the rest of the day. His Mum nudged him awake at six and ushered him upstairs. She knew his routine better than he did and didn't want him rushing around in a bad mood because he was late for meeting with his mates. A quick shower later and he was sat in the car awaiting the arrival of Symon, Sean and Sid. Jimmy stared blankly at the misted screen in front of him. There was a lot going through his head lately. He wasn't looking forward to explaining to the lads about the carb and how at £5 each a week it would take them ages to save up enough to buy a new part instead of the scrap part he thought he could get. The car had ended up costing them all a lot more than they had initially envisaged. It was still cheaper than they could have got a working one if they had taken out a loan and was it was probably still fair to say that it was the only way they would be able to own a car but it was disappointing for Jimmy and he knew the others would also be so. He shook himself out of his reverie and reached for the sponge. Wiping a sweeping curve across the mist he saw, bathed in the orange-yellow light of the street lamp, a girl waiting for the bus. He often saw her there and after about a year of minor investigations had found out that she worked down the road in a solicitors office and lived somewhere along Southmead Road.

The bus shushed to a stop, she got on and once again disappeared into the night. Symon, Sean and Sid walked round the corner has the diesel cloud from the departing bus slowly evaporated. En masse the three lads opened the doors and hopped in. After their usual greeting, Jimmy decided to broach the subject of the carburettor like a plaster on hairy skin. "Look. I went to the scrap yard today and ... well ... all the cars there have rusted, fucked carbs. I don't know what else to do. I can try and find another scrap yard somewhere. I hear there's one near Weston but I'll have to try and get a lift there or something. I'm real sorry lads. I didn't think we'd have this much trouble." Jimmy dropped his hands to his lap and looked down. Sid looked at him via the rear view mirror and spoke for all of them. "Hey now Jimmer! We all knew coming in that this was not a quick job. We're in it for the long haul. So it takes us another couple of months to get her going. No worries! I've got nowhere I wanna go anyway." Symon and Sean nodded agreement. "Yeah don't worry about it Jim." Sean reached forward and patted Jimmy's shoulder. "Thanks fellas. I promise I'll get something sorted soon as poss."

"So what's the plan for tonight boys?" Symon asked, looking around at the motley crew. "Well I'm broke. Apart from the £20 I've got for the carb." Jimmy mused. Sid reached into his pockets and pulled out fluff and a couple of tic tacs before shrugging. Sean patted his pockets. "Stoney." He sighed. The four lads sat there looking out of the windows.

"Right!" Jimmy finally said. "Time to go." He pretended to turn the key in the ignition and made the sound of the engine firing up. Pressing the clutch pedal and slipping the gearbox into first he started to slowly turn the steering wheel left and right as if manoeuvring. "Clifton here we come." Symon sat there just shaking his head. Jimmy turned the radio up just in time to hear DJ Ed Swarthy explain that he was covering the 'Saturday Slot' for a fellow DJ due to illness. He followed that with some wisecrack about frogs in throats before introducing "Walking on Sunshine by Katrina and the Waves". Jimmy looked across to the left and pointed, placing his outstretched arm right across Symon's face. "Look at them! Wow! Tops!

Now that's the kind of talent you only get round Clifton boys! I bet they're students. Reckon we should pull over and chat to them?" Unable to help themselves, the other three lads looked to the left where Jimmy was pointing. Jimmy turned the steering wheel to the left and gently brought the car to a stop. Sid, always one to join in with Jimmy, put his fingers to his mouth and whistled. He nudged Sean. "Open the window fella! I wanna chat to the ladies!" Sean pressed the down button on the door, tapped the door panel three times, stamped his foot twice and pressed the down button again. The window slowly, complainingly, descended. To keep everyone on their toes it sped up a couple of times and dropped more than moved the last couple of inches.

Sid leant across Sean and stuck his head out of the window. "Hello fair maidens." He welcomed them in his best attempt at a posh voice. "How fair thee this glorious evening?" He began to gently nod his head in response to their imagined reply, throwing in the odd "Fascinating!" at various stages of the conversation, for good measure. "The 'Studios' you say? Well no doubt myself and my fellow knights will perchance happen across that lugubrious watering hole and dance parlour sometime in the near future. I bid thee well." He doffed an imaginary cap and retreated into his seat. As Jimmy turned the steering wheel to the right and checked his mirrors before pulling away Symon turned to face Sid. "Oh you are SUCH a twat Sid!" He paused for full effect before continuing. "We want slappers not posh totty! Do you want to spend the evening buying bottles of wine and getting no further than a little over the jumper action in a student bedroom with her bunk mate lying there tutting and witness to you lasting no longer than 3 minutes from cacks down to job done?" Sid looked slack jawed at Symon and gently shook his head. "No course you don't! We need to find some slutalikes! Girls that will drop trow after three WKD blues and a good rendition of how you've just come back from Af and how brutal the fighting was over there and how frightened you are to be going back so soon and how nice it would be to just spend the night in the arms of a good old British girl. That's what we want!" Sean looked across at Sid in feigned disgust and punched him on the arm. "Twat!" He looked back out of his open window and reported. "Here we go boys! These are what we're looking for! Visible midriff, showing signs of getting that cute little winter bulge, high heels, belt for a skirt and ..." Sean feigned to look closer. "Yep! Carrying a bottle of Bud in their hand. Nature's leg opener! Pull over Jimmer, I'll sort us out." Jimmy pulled the car over and put the handbrake on. Sean nonchalantly leaned through the window. "Alright girls?

You're looking a bit cold there! Off to the Studios? Yeah we might swing by later. We've got to go meet some friends at some pre-concert 'do' at Colston Hall first. Who? Adam, Jesse, Mickey, Ryan and James ... they call themselves Maroon 5. You'd love to come? Sure, no problem. Hop in." Sean looked across at Sid. "Shove up Sid, make space for the girls." Everyone in the car burst into laughter as Sid shuffled over to the far side of the back seat. Jimmy looked back at Sean. "Maroon 5? We're mates with Maroon 5? They're from LA! How the hell did we get to be mates with THEM?! Now Portishead I could understand. It's plausible but Maroon 5? Knob!" Symon, in his usual laconic style turned to Jimmy. "This is a story where we're driving through Clifton in a car with no wheels, a duff engine and a bunch of fit girls swallow that we're somehow linked to the glitterati of modern pop music and decide to 'hop in the car' for Lord knows what frivolity on the way to backstage at the Colston Hall! Maroon 5 versus Portishead is the least of the problems with that story." Sean and Sid sat in the back chuckling to themselves. Trying to sound like he's just thought of it, Sean asked, "Ere Jimmer! Where's your sister tonight then?" Jimmy muttered, "Studios." Unable to hide his excitement, Sean replied, "Oh we gotta go!" then realising he had let his feelings out of the bag, "I still reckon I got a chance with her, bud!" Jimmy, Symon and

Bristle

Sid shared a look. All three of them in unison chanted, "What chance has he got? Norfolk and Chance!" before falling about laughing. Sean's face dropped in offence. Jimmy turned to face Sean. "Listen mate. Firstly, she's gone to a night club and we don't have money, shoes, trousers or transport. Secondly, she's got a boyfriend now, with a job. Thirdly, you touch her and I'll smack you and finally, you're THE ugliest fucker I've ever seen. K?" Symon paused briefly before adding, "Harsh! But true." Sean replied, "'Ang on a mo! I've got shoes and trousers! Do I LOOK like I came out in my grundies and bare feet?" With a smile on his face, Jimmy answered, "Yeah but they ain't PROPER shoes and trousers, ya dork! You can't go into the Studios wearing fake Nike trainers and jeans." Looking even more horrified, Sean replied, "Who says they're fake?" Chuckling, Symon answered, "The fact that they say *Mike* not *Nike* is a big clue!" Joining in, Sid added, "**And** ya jeans say *Wangler*!"

Slowly the mood changed as the four lads sat idly masticating on their own thoughts. Eventually Jimmy spoke. "Problem is ..." Symon filled in the pause. "Go on Jimmer." Jimmy took a deep breath. "The problem is that it seems all we have are dreams. I know I'm a little down about the car ..." Sid interjected "and having no girlfriend and not having the guts to speak to bus-stop girl"

28

Jimmy stared at him through the rear view mirror "but we appear to be months away from fixing it, if at all. NONE of us has a girlfriend. Probably some of us have never actually been with a girl at all!" Jimmy pointedly looked at Sid. "I love my job but can't see much of a future in it. I don't see how college is going to change anything. I haven't travelled outside of Bristol in ten years and only then to Minehead for shitty caravan holidays. Are any of us working toward our dreams? Do we all actually have dreams?" Symon, looking down at his hands clasped in his lap, retorted "I've got a dream!" Jimmy shook his head. "Professional footballer? No you haven't Sly. It's little more than an option in your head." Symon's face turned red with anger. "What the hell do you mean? I left home to pursue this dream!" Jimmy calmly replied "Yes you did leave home but was that not more because you wanted to leave home than you desperately needed to be a footballer? You smoke, drink, partake of the wacky-backy. You're late for training most days and aren't first pick for the rezzies never mind knocking on the door of the first team. Is your heart really in it?" Symon's jaw moved up and down involuntarily as his mind tried to formulate a response but eventually he realised the truth in Jimmy's words and closed his mouth, looking down again at his hands. Sean stared out of the window. "It looks like Mum & Dad are going to have to sell the farm. We had a bad year with the crops and milk prices have been going down and down. I overheard them arguing the other night. Mum asked Dad if the stress was really worth it any more. Dad broke down. I've never seen him cry before. He kept mumbling 'I'm a farmer. I don't know nothing else.' Not sure what that means for me. I was earmarked to take over from him one day like he did from his Dad and his Dad did from his." Jimmy looked at Sid. "What about you One-ton?" Without looking up Sid replied quietly. "Dunno. BAe I spose. Mum and Dad work there. All my aunts and uncles work there or Rolls Royce. Even as far back as when the site was the Bristol Aeroplane Company my family worked there. Our house isn't painted Concorde white for fun! So yeah, I guess British Aerospace is my future." Sean looked across at him. "Wife and two kids? Work for your annual fortnight in Benidorm till retirement then swap the Filton site for the allotments till your heart gives out?" Still not looking up Sid replied, "Yup I guess. Obviously some part of me wants more but the chances of me being picked up by MI5 and becoming the next James Bond are pretty slim. So what choice do I actually have? It's only people who have achieved their dreams that tell you how life is not limited by your environment. For every one of them, there are a million who look at them through green goggles. Every actor needs a paying audience." The silence returned to the car and the four lads just sat there. Finally Symon spoke. "I'm offski. See you at college on Monday." Sean and Sid mumbled their goodbyes and the three of them left Jimmy idly polishing the dash.

Bristle

Golden Showers

Monday morning came quicker than Jimmy had hoped. He'd spent Sunday fruitlessly trying to fix some of the myriad electrical faults on the car and wondering if there was any way he could fix the faulty carb rather than buy a replacement but to no avail. He got showered and dressed on autopilot and ambled slowly to college, still arriving before anybody else. As he stood outside the metalwork room leaning against the wall, one of the other lads from the course, Terry Wanstrow, came rushing out through the door and bundled into him. Picking himself up then reaching out to help Jimmy up, Terry couldn't hide the huge grin on his face and realising that Jimmy might recognise he had been up to no good, lifted his finger to his lips and said "Shhh. Mum's, OK?" Jimmy knew nothing anyway so nodded agreement.

Terry disappeared, not returning until everybody else was there queuing up for Mr Graeme "hey man" Stewartson to open the room. Finally "hey man" showed up and greeted them all with his usual hippy-esque greeting. "Hey guys! Cool day to meld metal!" he oozed as he fished his keys from his pocket and unlocked the door. Jimmy was confused. Either half the class had suddenly developed a really keen interest in metalwork over the weekend or they knew something he didn't. They all pressed together in a crowd and pushed forward into the room right behind Mr Stewartson. As was his daily routine, on entering the room Mr Stewartson flicked the power switch that was on the wall just inside the door. This sent electricity coursing through the chunky 3-phase wiring to the 12 lathes that formed an avenue along the central aisle of the room, with sturdy wooden benches spurring off to either side. Each lathe had a small plastic tube which delivered a steady flow of orangey-yellow cooling lubricant to the point of contact between the cutting tool and whatever was being cut. Someone had increased the flow of the lubricant and adjusted the tubing so that instead of pointing directly at the cutting tool, each actually pointed up and toward the central aisle. As the power reached the lathes, 12 majestically beautiful arcs of golden fluid plumed into the air to form a glittering tunnel of cooling lubricant. Mr Stewartson panicked. As the sight of these 12 arcs hit him, his immediate reaction was to turn each tube back to its intended target. As he rushed forward and reached for the first lathe, his feet met the puddle of golden lubricant and chose to see what the view was like at eye level. His head hit the ground with a loud thud but not hard enough to do any real damage. This did not knock any sense into him though, instead he flailed around like a spider on roller skates skidding on hands and knees from lathe to lathe trying to turn the tubes back to their intended position. Eventually one of the lads, who had all been watching in astonished and silent shock and horror, reached across and flicked off the power. The 12 golden arcs drooped from their former glory until they slowly dribbled out of existence. Mr Stewartson lay in the middle of the aisle covered in lubricant from head to toe. It coated his hair and face and filled his ears. His clothing was dark from the drenching fluid. A slow guttural whisper began deep in his throat rising steadily until it became one long shouted "GOOOOOOOOOOOOOOOOOOOOOOOOO!" As the lads turned to leave all they could hear were the broken mutterings of the worst language ever to come out of Goven, his birthplace, which despite his efforts to neutralise his accent, always returned in moments such as these. Every other word was an expletive or a body part. Deciding that college was done for the day, Jimmy, Symon, Sean and Sid opted for the pub leaving Mr Stewartson to ... 'cool' down.

Bristle

Septic

Jimmy lay in bed with his laptop open lying on his legs. He and 'Princess Alicia' were wandering round the virtual world hand in hand. It was possible to have virtual sex in this make believe world and though interesting in the early days it soon paled in excitement. For all the beautiful graphics and the wonderfully crafted animation and scenery, those who had been members of this world for longer than a couple of months spent most of their time just talking. And so it was between Jimmy or 'Studly' and 'Princess Alicia'. He had explained his life in England and described in detail his family and friends. She had told him all about her life and how she had a young daughter and an ex-husband who was so far out of the picture he wasn't even in the same state. They spoke most evenings and more so on the weekends. In the virtual world they were virtual man and wife which again was more to experience the virtual ceremony than for any higher or more romantic reasons. Tonight they had talked mainly about some of the internal politics of the game and briefly about how they both felt their real lives were in a rut. Jimmy had mentioned that his Mum and Dad were going down to Minehead for a couple of days stay in a caravan and that it was something about 'finding the spark' but that he had paid very little attention to the conversation. Jimmy also didn't understand why this snippet of news had piqued Princess Alicia's interest so much but again he paid it very little attention. Jimmy started to yawn as his bedside clock ticked past 2am and making his excuses logged off. Deciding it to be a good idea to have a pee before bedtime he wandered into the bathroom and stood prepared. Waiting for his body to send the message to his bladder to start pushing he heard the sound of voices outside. He tried to peer out of the window but the frosted glass and the distance of the toilet from the window combined to make it impossible for him to see or hear more than that it was raised voices, though he recognised one as his sister Vickie. The conversation seemed to understand the volume of his pee hitting the toilet water as it rose substantially. He was able to pick out individual words but no complete sentences. Vickie said "Pig" and a few other choice swear words while her counterpart had said something involving the word "own" and "relax". It was all very confusing. Then the conversation changed again and he sensed that Vickie had become the calm one while whoever she was speaking to had become very angry. As Jimmy shook himself dry he contemplated going down to see what was happening but was saved by the sound of the door slamming shut. He paused for a second before leaving the bathroom. He stepped out onto the landing just as his sister reached the top of the stairs.

Shocking Jimmy to his core, Vickie burst into tears and threw herself into his arms. He just wrapped himself around her and let her cry. After a while a few words began to intermingle with her sobbing but similarly to her argument he could barely discern any real meaning behind them. Instead he just gave her a bit of a squeeze and said "You're really keen on this guy aren't you, Vix?" She said nothing, just nodded into his shoulder. "One question sis, what makes him deserving of you?" Her sobbing immediately began to die down. Eventually she looked up at Jimmy with a quizzical expression. "I dunno. I just love him." Showing wisdom beyond his years and previously invisible even to himself Jimmy just nodded and replied "Even loves comes at a cost Vix. Just make sure you rate yourself high enough to get value for money." Vickie smiled at Jimmy and though she didn't immediately get the full meaning of what he was saying, she let him go and walked into her room throwing a "Thanks Jimmer" behind her along with a cloud of perfume. Jimmy returned to his bedroom and flopped onto his bed. He lay awake for a while thinking about Vickie until his eyes finally shut.

The next morning Jimmy woke a little later than usual and had to rush to make sure he was standing outside ready for Paul to pick him up in the van. There was no sign of

Vickie as she had to get the early bus into the city centre. She worked at John Lewis on the perfume counter. It was a job renowned for being filled by the most attractive girls and Vickie fitted it perfectly. Standing outside, running a cloth over the bonnet of the car while he waited for Paul, Jimmy suddenly noticed the girl at the bus stop. His heart rate immediately sky rocketed and a million thoughts appeared in his mind vying for attention. "I should go over and say hello.", "Stay here polishing the car.", "Look over from time to time to see if she looks this way.", "Yeah and be ready to nod a nonchalant 'Hi' if she does.", "Keep your head down – she's too good for you." Surprisingly, the most radical thought actually won out which was perhaps testament to how much he fancied her. He tossed the rag into the car and slammed the door loudly. He walked over to the bus stop and stood next to her. "Hi. I'm Jimmy. I've seen you waiting here before." She turned to him and smiled. "Finally, my own stalker!" she joked. Jimmy turned even redder than he already was but smiled. "Oh definitely! I've been stalking you for months! Yet your name escapes me." Not realising it until going over this conversation in his head later that day, Jimmy was impersonating Paul, his boss. She smiled at the fairly blunt attempt but responded favourably. "Jennifer." Jimmy proffered his hand and replied "James. Pleased to meet you." She took it delicately and shook it. At that moment the bus appeared at the end of the road. Jennifer turned to Jimmy and said "Nice to meet you too, James. Perhaps we'll meet again." Suddenly stuck for words, Jimmy just smiled and watched her get on the bus and disappear. Thankfully he didn't have long to well in his inept display of wordsmithery as Paul's van followed immediately behind the bus. Jimmy hopped in with a scowl on his face and mumbled a greeting to his boss. "And a good morning to you too, young Jimmy." He replied.

They were working in Swindon today and it was halfway along the M4 before Jimmy's mood picked up enough for him to engage in the previously one-sided conversation with Paul. Jimmy had just finished explaining the encounter with Jennifer when they arrived at the shop that needed a new window (bless those vandals) and some new vinyl signage. Between the occasional instruction, Paul told Jimmy that he should congratulate himself on making the move with Jennifer. "It would have been so much easier to make an excuse like 'the timing's not right' but the truth is that the timing is always right when the opportunity arises. One thing you need to understand is that your mind is acting like one conversation with Jennifer will lead to dating, sex, a relationship, marriage, kids etc etc and that the weight of all that expectation lies on a single action. Those men who are 'good with women' are those that are natural and relaxed with women. Those are the men who see each conversation as simply that and no more. What will come, will come and only when it comes does it become necessary to think about it." Jimmy smiled at this imparted wisdom and decided then and there to be more relaxed about the whole thing, if he could. Glass replaced and signage in place, Jimmy and Paul got back in the van and began the return journey to Bristol. The next job was in The Galleries which meant a difficult transition through walking crowds in order to get the van near the shop. Jimmy mentioned his experience with Vickie the night before. Paul listened intently and playfully punched him on the arm at the end, saying, "You're a good brother. Saying nothing when nothing needs to be said then saying just the right thing when something does is a difficult skill James, and you've got it." Jimmy smiled at this. Praise from anyone was nice but from someone whose opinion matters to him counted greatly. The conversation turned to idle chat and Jimmy mentioned that his folks were going to Minehead. "Relight my fire!" Paul sang out loud, much to Jimmy's surprise. Paul giggled. "Sorry. So they are rekindling eh? Good for them!" Jimmy looked at Paul with a frown. "You're parents have been together for quite a well yes?" Jimmy nodded. "Well things can get stagnant between a couple, especially when there are children about. A couple of days alone with nothing to do but explore the bed and each other could work wonders." Jimmy's face turned to horror. "You mean they're shagging? They're going away for a dirty midweeker! Ewwww!" Paul laughed. "Of course they are! And why not? Do you really think the desire for sex dies when you reach 30? Seriously James!" Jimmy still looked horrified. "Way too much information!"

Sid sat down with his family for his favourite meal, Sunday lunch. On this occasion it was roast pork, roast potatoes, carrots, cabbage, gravy and lashings of apple sauce. He wolfed it down in record time and was halfway through 'seconds' when he felt a rumble in his stomach. Initially he thought nothing of it until the rumble became a grumble which slowly moved lower through his body until he felt the pressure against his sphincter. Assuming his body had reacted positively and perfectly correctly to a little pocket of trapped wind, Sid applied a little intestinal pressure and ... "Oh crap! I've followed through!" he shouted as he clenched his legs together and rushed for the stairs to the toilet. Performing a waddle of which a penguin would be proud he pounded up the stairs while still clenching his buttocks and holding his stomach. On arriving in the lavatory he struggled briefly with his belt buckle, jeans button and zip

Bristle

before, in one fluid movement, pushing his combined trousers and undies down while backing up and crouching on the toilet. There he encountered two issues. The first and probably least of his worries was that he hadn't quite timed it perfectly and had started to 'issue forth' from his nether regions prior to being fully over the toilet. But the second and clinically fatal error was that in his haste he had completely neglected to lift the toilet lid. So there he sat with a pool of effluence puddling between his buttocks and thighs forming a cascading muddy-brown waterfall over the edge of the seat. It was at this moment that a further issue came to his attention.

His stomach was moaning for attention and as the beads of sweat formed on his brow he felt the bile rising in his throat. His only option was the bath in front of him so he leaned forward and opened his mouth wide. Full bore the contents of his stomach erupted from his wide-stretched mouth and splashed into the olive green bath tub. This effort sadly released other muscle groups and his bowels let forth the remainder of their contents in an equally impressive fountain. It was at this moment that he caught sight, in the corner of his eye, of in image in the bathroom mirror that would scar him for life. There, reflected in the mirror, was a fat adolescent with a tight fitting T-shirt, trousers round his ankles, hair matted with sweat, puke dribbling from his mouth and shit pumping from his backside. In that single moment Sid began the process of dieting that would become a lifelong obsession. To a degree this obsession relied principally on the irrational fear of such an occasion reoccurring and morphed into a belief that 'if it wasn't in him it couldn't come spewing out of him' but in reality it turned him into a person who only ate in small amounts and only when hungry. It would, over the next year turn him into a lithe, if not perhaps a little skinny, grazer. He never ate pork again. But for now he was left crumpled on the floor, covered in most of the outpourings a body can produce, whimpering to himself.

His mother, concerned for him, poked her head around the door and instantly regretted it. But being his flesh and blood, she took control. She bade him remove his clothes and get in the shower. Meanwhile she began to clear up the mess, using the bath as a temporary waste receptacle for the three toilet rolls it took to mop up the floor. A couple of black bin bags and two full bottles of bleach later and Sid was lying in his bed with a towel underneath him and one on his lap. A bucket sat waiting beside the bed 'just in case'. He slowly drifted off to sleep ever grateful to his Mum but the diet seed had been sown and was slowly germinating while he dreamt of river rafting on a chocolate river, strangely enough, without a paddle.

That night, Jimmy decided to stay in and chat to Princess Alicia, Sid was indisposed which left Symon and Sean with nothing much to do. Symon had received a goal bonus from last month so suggested to Sean that they go out and celebrate. They donned their best jeans, shirts and trainers and set out for the nearest pub with live music because, as Symon portended "All the fit girls like music." He somehow neglected to contemplate that all the ugly ones did too. The beat of the music hit them before they saw the bright lights of the pub. There was a definite buzz around the place and the two lads fairly skipped into the cacophony and throbbing lights of the gig.

Symon got to the bar first and ordered four pints, two each, to save queuing again. They found a space in the corner and listened to the band performing the third song in their set. "What's this band called?" Sean shouted to Symon. "Wotsits and balled?" Symon questioned. "What's this band called?" Sean shouted louder, this time right into Symon's ear. "Oh! 'Nieces of Necrophilia', I think!" He replied. Thinking that would explain the high percentage of Goth looking girls, Sean continued nodding away to himself while scoping for talent. A tall girl dressed in black leather with a long cloak strode purposefully up to Symon, whispered something in his ear, turned and walked away. Symon looked at Sean, shrugged and followed. "Fuck!" thought Sean. "He's pulled!" This made Sean even more determined to, as his Dad would say, 'put himself about a bit', though he doubted his father was really the hit with the ladies he portrayed. His father always hastened to add "Before your mother snared me and turned me onto the wonderful life of mahogany I now live." Sean didn't have the heart to correct him.

Sean saw a gaggle of girls hanging round the front of the stage (a description oozing in poetic licence) and decided to mosey over and see if he could snag a straggler. After five minutes of dancing near them but never quite getting eye contact, he decided to go back to the bar and get a rum and coke down his neck. Standing there with his fiver in his outstretched hand, trying to get the barman's attention, he suddenly realised someone was staring at him. He turned round to find an Amazonian girl in a flouncy, flowery dress stood there with her face no more than 6 inches from his. Leaning back he smiled nervously at her. She motioned for him to follow her so he did. She waltzed outside and out to the front of the pub. In the relative quiet of the front beer garden she sat at a table and motioned for him to join her. He introduced himself and asked her name.

Bristle

"Sara." She replied. "I saw you checking out all the ladies. Looks like I've bagged myself a player!" Stumbling through his denial Sean replied, "No! Not at all! Just my first time listening to this band. Ummm. Wanted the full experience! They were no better close up! Haha." His nervous laughter did little to relax his mood. "I live nearby but I'm afraid of the dark so would you be a gentleman and walk me home?" Sean might have come across as pretty naive but even he saw this as a good turning point in the evening's activities. "Oh, uh, with pleasure." She got up and crooked her arm. Sean put his through hers and followed her lead.

They walked about three houses down from the pub and turned into what had been in its heyday a large Victorian house but was now converted into a mish-mash of student bedsits. As she unlocked the front door all the lights inside the hall and up the stairs turned on automatically. Sara didn't relax her hold on his arm and moved up the stairs. Sean began to have his doubts. This was all far too easy. The sense of being a powerful lion, king of the jungle began to fade as the image of being a male black widow spider took its place. As they reached the top of the stairs and Sara opened her door, Sean paused and pulled away from her. "Umm. Well here you go. Safe and sound. I'll be off then." Inside he was kicking himself. He was blowing it just because she was a strong minded woman who knew what she wanted and was not afraid to go after it! Or at least that's what one part of his mind was shouting. Just because she knew what she wanted and for some reason what she wanted was him, he was throwing away this clear chance of sex! Not only that but sex with a gorgeous looking woman. Agreed she was a big girl but one with all the right bits in all the right places and in truth wonderfully proportioned. She truly did embody the Amazon look. "Well surely you must be tired? Why don't you stay the night? I've got a double bed." Sara asked. Something inside him clicked and he realised he was not going to run from this. She wanted him and who was he to rebuff her? "Sure." He acquiesced. "No funny business though!" Sara stated. Confusing though her last comment was, it actually relaxed Sean. "No funny business?" he thought. "Well what the hell are we playing at then?" While Sara preened herself at an ornate antique dressing table, Sean quickly got undressed and slipped into the bed as close to the edge as possible. Sara turned to Sean and moved up close. "No looking!" she said as in one movement, giving Sean no chance to react or look away, she gripped her dress by the hem and swooshed it over her head. Slack jawed Sean lay there looking at her wearing dark black stockings, suspender belt, no panties or bra but a smirking smile. She slid under the covers and

Bristle

manoeuvred herself under Sean. Elbows propping himself up and taking most of his body weight he began to kiss her lips. They were soft and moist and nicely fleshy. He felt her legs wrap around his body and pull him closer. He kissed slowly down her neck until he felt the softness of her breast under his lips. Her hard erect nipple grazed his cheek. "Let me tell you a story." Sara interrupted. "What now?" Sean questioned. "There was this guy who had sex with this girl and she fell pregnant." She continued. "She told everyone he raped her and he got put away for it." Sean, now resting on one elbow while looking at her in confusion, replied "And the moral to this story is?" Sara shook her head. "Oh nothing." The blood drained from Sean's face and other extremities enabling it to return to his brain. He rolled off her and out of bed. He stood into and pulled up his jeans and undies, slipped his feet into his shoes and pulled on his T-shirt. Buckling his belt he walked to the door, took a final look back at Sara, who by this time had pulled back the covers to leave her lying there providing a most inviting picture, shook his head, shuddered and left.

He spent the entire walk home going over the events of that evening in his head. He considered every move he made and every word he said. He thought hard about her story and still couldn't get his head around it.

By the time he arrived home he was positive that he probably missed out on the best sex of his life but that staying out of jail made it totally worth it.

Symon followed the leather clad woman outside. She didn't pause until she reached her car and got in. Unsure what to do Symon stood beside the passenger door until she looked up at him from inside and motioned for him to join her. The door opened and he sat inside. She fired up the engine and headed off towards the downs. Symon was confused. He was not exactly naive or inexperienced when it came to women. As a good-looking, fit, semi-professional footballer he was used to a little limelight and getting 'picked up' by women was not new to him but this seemed very different. This seemed like a totally different rodeo. He attempted some small talk. "I'm Symon, what's your name?" She kept looking forward. "We'll get to that." The car turned into the driveway of a large house whose gates opened automatically and closed behind them. They drove down a long drive lined by mature oak trees with what seemed to be, from what Symon could make out in the dark, manicured lawns either side. They pulled up to the front of a huge house with pillars either side of a long stone staircase. She got out and walked straight up the stairs where the door opened and a well dressed man greeted her. This stopped

Bristle

Symon in his tracks. He was used to an audience when he played football but as far as he was concerned, sex was not a spectator sport. The gentleman greeted her as she dropped her coat over his arm and her gloves and keys on the silver platter he proffered. "Good evening Mistress." The man looked towards Symon. "Sir? Will you come this way please?" Symon paused before accepting the invitation. His mind was awash with some very disconcerting thoughts but another part of his anatomy was in decision mode and won out. He climbed the stairs slowly and walked inside, followed by the gentleman. Inside the door the girl stood by a small table which held a bottle of champagne and two glasses. "Welcome to my home Symon. You've met Jenkins, my butler. He will be retiring soon." Symon looked across at him. "Seems a bit young to retire." Jenkins having disposed of her gloves, coat and keys appeared by the table and began pouring two glasses of champagne. The girl picked up a glass and offered it to Symon who tentatively took and sipped it. It seemed, to his limited palate, like champagne. "My name is Mistress Donna. If you decide to take me up on my offer, you will call me Mistress." Symon took another sip of champagne. "And what exactly is it that you are offering?" She smiled. "I am offering an experience for which many would and have paid a small fortune. I will open your eyes to a world few get to see but many long for. I will drain you of every ounce of ... well let's leave that for later." Symon, for some reason, was interested but still confused. "I'm listening." She continued. "You will need to sign a contract, for the safety of everybody concerned. It is a simple contract that simply states you are here of your own free will and that everything that occurs is consensual. It lays out rules to which I must and will adhere. It provides you with the means to protect yourself and limit me." The sunlight slowly peeked over the hills of his confusion. "Ahhh! You are my Mistress Grey?" She nodded. "Though I've always felt that perhaps fifty shades of BLUE is a more apt description of what we will be ... contemplating." Symon reflected on this. "I have no desire to get tied up and beaten. I'm up for sex and the kinkier the better but I face enough pain playing football." Mistress Donna shook her head. "Oh please don't misunderstand me. That is entirely the purpose. I want to show you a world of pleasure that you have not even come close to in the past. The 'punishment' is purely a means to heighten the experience." She picked up a single sheet of paper from the table and passed it to him. "Read the contract. If you agree, sign it and Jenkins will bring you to me. I will place a ring on your finger which is my symbol of collaring. Many powerful and influential people wear my collar. If you do not agree, Jenkins will drive you home." She turned and walked past the ornate sweeping staircase to an old oak door. It creaked as it opened. She disappeared inside, descending down into the darkness. "Would you like a seat while you read Sir?" Jenkins offered. Symon sat down and began to look over the page. He read a long list of rules and regulations followed by two bullet lists of commitments. On the left of the page, titled 'Mistress' were items such as 'Honours the gift' and 'Protects' while on the right of the page, titled 'Submissive' were items such as 'Obeys without question' and 'Worships'. Symon finished reading both sides of the page and sat thinking. A question sprang up in his mind and he quickly scanned the document and found the answer. He slowly read the page again. Jenkins stood nearby silently, patiently waiting. What was offered to Symon by this strange and mysterious woman was an experience. Symon was not short on experiences. The nature of a professional footballer, even an apprentice was one filled with experiences. There's nothing like a little fame, fit body, good looks and youth to provide an increase in opportunities to indulge in the seedier side of life. Symon was no virgin. He had even been propositioned by and succumbed to the advances of twins but even that paled into insignificance before the experience offered to him tonight. Life is too short to regret missed chances but why risk regret when you can take those chances and at least look in hindsight from a position of experience rather than a position of ignorance. He signed the sheet of paper and handed it to Jenkins. He stood and followed Jenkins to a door near the stairs. Jenkins punched a number into the keypad and waited for Symon to walk inside. The door closed behind him leaving Jenkins on the other side. Symon's eyes quickly became accustomed to the dark red glow of the light in the corridor which, he realised, ran for about twenty feet before descending down a long flight of stairs to another door. He walked carefully down the stairs and entered a dimly lit changing room with a further door on the far side which was, on testing it, locked. It seemed clear, without need for instruction, that he should remove his clothes. He did so, hanging them over the back of a plush armchair. As soon as his last item of clothing hit the chair, a loud click sounded and the door opened. Wearing nothing but a smile, he walked through it and found himself in a room that other than a path of circular lights on the floor was completely dark. He followed the path through what he could just about make out was a collection of devices of various sizes and shapes. As he neared the end of the lit path, a spotlight turned on revealing a throne in which sat Mistress Donna. She looked at Symon with a faint smile on her face. She held a crop in one hand which she playfully

Bristle

tapped against her other hand. She motioned for Symon to stop which he did. She stood up enabling Symon to see her full outfit. She was dressed in a black leather bustier which barely covered her nipples, allowing a good portion of her areolae air. Below that long black stockings started just below black silk French knickers and hugged her long legs till they met ankle high black leather boots. As Symon's eyes looked her up and down she smiled and began to walk around him returning the inspection. As she did so she traced the tip of her riding crop along the contours of his body. Symon stood still and to attention allowing Mistress Donna to continue without interruption. She tossed her crop onto the chair and disappeared into the dark momentarily, returning with some rope and other devices, none of which were instantly recognisable to Symon. She began to slowly tie his hands and arms together behind him. She then pressed a button on a remote control and another light came on illuminating a red leather padded table to which she steered Symon. The evening took many turns from that point with Symon reaching highs and lows in equal measure. It ended with Symon and Mistress Donna lying naked on a massive silk sheeted bed. Mistress Donna had her arms wrapped around the sleeping figure of Symon as if protecting him from the world.

Jimmy awoke on Wednesday morning and remembering that he had a couple of days off (Paul was away at a conference) and that his Mum and Dad were away in Minehead, he starfished under his duvet and pulled his pillow around his head to settle in for another hours snooze. Not hearing it initially, he recognised the rumble of the vibration before he lifted his head and heard his phone ring. Reaching across to his bedside table he answered it sleepily. "Yup?" There was a brief pause at the other end. "Jimmy?" A female voice with a very different accent questioned him. "Is that you?" Still confused, Jimmy replied. "Yes, who's this?" Another pause. "It's Princess Alicia, Studly!" Jimmy was suddenly wide awake. "How did you get my number?" The American accent on the other end of the phone replied, "You gave it to me months ago but we never got round to talking on it as we both had Skype." Realisation dawned on Jimmy. "Oh right. Yeah I remember. So to what do I owe this surprise pleasure?" Jimmy relaxed a little. "Well I have another surprise for you, Studly. I'm at Heathrow Airport. Can you come pick me up?" Jimmy sat bolt upright. "You're what? Umm. I haven't got a car! Umm." Sweat poured off his forehead. "OK. I'll get the train or a coach. Speak to you soon." She hung up. Jimmy got out of bed and began a process of pacing that would last most of the day. "Oh my God, oh my God, oh my God." This mantra failed to help his mind get away from the immediate panic and anxiety that poured through him. The cotton wool of confusion filled his head, drenched by the flood of fear and overpowered by the smell of anticipation. Suddenly he stopped pacing. "She's flown thousands of miles, to see me!" He drew the curtains and looked out of the window. "I'm going to have sex!" He began pacing again. Three hours passed and he had done little more than pace and repeat himself. The phone rang. She was at the bus station in Bristol. He gave her his address and hung up. He rushed to the window and stared out wondering from which direction her taxi would come. He then suddenly remembered that he hadn't showered, dressed or tidied his room. He rushed into the bathroom, grabbed his toothbrush, toothpaste, shaving foam and razor and hopped into the shower. Surviving the initial cold water onslaught he managed to wash himself, clean his teeth and shave in record time. The aftershave that he splashed all over his face informed him that he had shaved far too quickly. He dressed rapidly as he had a very limited wardrobe of what he could call his 'best'. He rushed around tidying the room and moved back to the window. During his shower he had worked out that a taxi coming from the Bus station would come up the road from the left so he concentrated his gaze in that direction. He opened a window to allow the cold air to dry his fevered brow and stop his armpits from colouring his underarms with sweat. Car after car came round the corner. Then the strangest sight appeared. A beat-up old brown Nissan came round the corner spitting sparks from its back end like a Catherine wheel. "Sheesh! How can a taxi driver" ... "Oh my God it's a Taxi!" ... "drive a car with a busted axle?" The scraping sound screamed through the window getting louder as it neared. The cars behind it were keeping their distance and sped past when the taxi indicated to pull over in front of Jimmy's house. The driver got out and opened the rear door. Slowly a head appeared above the roof of the car as the whole car bounced up like a weight lifter dropping the barbell. A loud creak was the equivalent of the vehicle sighing as the pressure on its springs eased. The taxi driver closed the door and opened the boot obscuring the view as he retrieved his passenger's suitcase. Slowly, inexorably, horrifically, his passenger rounded the car and took the case from the driver. Looking straight at Jimmy she smiled and walked towards the front door. "What the fuck!? Oh my God!" Jimmy froze. "She's flown thousands of miles!" He walked slowly out of his room and down the stairs. "I can't send her home!" He opened the door and took her case from her outstretched hand. She pressed forward and turned sideways but still scraped both sides of the doorway as she came into the house. Jimmy dropped her case at the foot of the stairs. "Cup of Tea?" he asked behind him as he walked towards the kitchen. "Coffee please." It was not a small kitchen but it was filled with Jimmy and Alicia. He made her coffee while sneaking occasional looks at her. He had Skyped her and found her incredibly pretty. And in truth, if he put his fingers and thumbs together like a film director and framed just her head and shoulders, she WAS a VERY pretty girl. But oh what the camera obscured! He looked down her neck and her shoulders flattened out and just kept going. Where his might have ended, hers went on and on. Then they rounded off to house the biggest arms Jimmy had ever seen. His grandmother was a woman who had worked hard all her life and he thought her arms were huge but in comparison they were skin and bone. Alicia's body had no curves to speak of other than one huge curve from neck to ankle. Jimmy was acutely aware that she had come all this way and he hadn't given her a hug or shown her any affection whatsoever and as time crept on it nearly overpowered her as the only elephant in the room. Gripping the plaster, as it were, he moved over to her and hugged her. He was no runt himself but his arms couldn't actually reach all the way round her, falling short somewhere around mid shoulder blade. Looking into her eyes he could see the spark of inner beauty that most people have and perhaps this helped him lean forward and kiss her. Her lips opened and her tongue pushed inside and filled his mouth. Nearly gagging on the stale coffee breath of a nearly 4000 mile journey he pulled away. Alicia looked at him and smiled. "C'mon Studly. Take me to bed." For some reason this caused an unwanted reaction in Jimmy. He wretched but managed to hide it well. Alicia took his hand and led him to the stairs. Turning sideways she scraped herself between the wall and the banister which had to sway uneasily to one side until she burst onto the landing. Realising he was not going to be able to push past her Jimmy helped by saying. "First on the right." Following her inside he arrived just in time to find her stand at the foot of the bed, turn and fall backwards. The black humorist within Jimmy shouted "Timberrrrrr!" and then shuddered as he watched the folds of fat on her stomach ripple like a tsunami, flowing inexorably down to her giant redwood-like legs. He experienced a brief out of body moment as he looked down on the scene without emotion. Clinically he assessed her thighs to be bigger than his waist and her waist bigger than two of him. Strangely, for all her size, she was incredibly limber, he realised as she deftly pulled her top off and shucked her stretchy bottoms. She rolled to one side as her hand moved behind her back and unclipped her bra. She smiled the smile of those who are immensely proud

Bristle

of something and expecting a big reaction when placing that thing on public show. As she shrugged it from her shoulders and revealed her massive mammaries Jimmy was pondering how on earth she was going to remove those panties and partly hoping she couldn't and would give up. He didn't have to wait long as she reached to the sides and pulled on small ribbons that undid the sides of her knickers. Pulling on the front she slid them between her thighs, no mean feat in itself, and starfished on the bed in her full naked glory. Again, Jimmy held back a wretch. Suddenly his mind turned northern comedian and flooded with a million fat girl jokes. Cover her in flour and look for the dark spot. Slap her thigh and ride the wave in. One after another the jokes sprang to mind. Tie a plank to your feet. Remember your scuba gear. The problem was that he was looking down at her thinking that in fact a pound of flour would prove extremely useful at this point as the folds of flab from her stomach and thighs obliterated any view of ... the target. Clearly the point of no return had long past and Jimmy had come to terms with the fact that he was going to 'take one for the team'. He knelt between her legs though it was a squeeze to even do that. He worked out a plan in his mind. He would start at the point nearest him and work up. There was no space above her waist so he had little choice. He angled his arm like someone digging a toothbrush out of the toilet bowl and dove in. He wiggled his fingers and explored the depths like Lewis and Clark, mentally mapping his route as he went. Eureka! He found moisture! Hmmm. A lot of moisture. More cream than moisture. Oh that's a lot of cream. And then the smell hit him. His involuntary wretch returned. It may have been something more repugnant but Jimmy assumed that the 4000 mile trip was the culprit and principal bad guy in the production of this copious amount of almost glutinous fluid. He found that if he went at the task with three fingers he could use two to pry apart the folds of fat while the third explored. Using this technique he found a spot that elicited several groans and copious amounts of frothing, pungent cream. He added his other hand and like a vet putting all his effort into delivering a particularly stubborn calf, he dove in with gusto. Thinking it best to remain at a point of some success rather than strain for more and risk losing what he had worked so hard to achieve, Jimmy continued poking whatever it was beneath his outstretched finger while his other hand continued to desperately hold back the folds of flab threatening to overcome his manual dam and flood forth breaking several bones in the process. At this point, Alicia reached down and grabbed her inner thighs forcing them apart while screaming "Fuck me Jimmy! Fuck me!" Jimmy contemplated why she had not done this trick with her thighs earlier and allowed him better access to whatever it was he was touching but the moment passed as he realised what he was being bidden to do next. He pulled his arms away with a loud slurping noise and stood before her. He slowly removed his clothes hoping that the extensively eked out striptease looked like he was putting on a show rather than the more truthful postponement of an inevitable but unwanted event. He threw his last piece of clothing to the floor and knelt once again between her legs. He pushed his hips between her thighs. He was no 'king' in the 'dong' department but surprised himself at how easily the end of his manhood found its target and pushed inside. Alicia grunted loudly and moaned as Jimmy pumped back and forth like a demented miner. Being now laid across her chest he believed he was in a position to nibble her nipples but found that even stretching his neck as far as possible he could barely stick his tongue out far enough to traverse the dinner plate sized areola. It mattered not as at that moment she chose to participate and with both hands grabbed her breast and man-handled it into her own mouth. She suckled on it like a hungry infant. The sweat poured off Jimmy like a waterfall as he pushed back and forth again and again. It was a surprising sign to him of how long it had been since he had been with a woman that he managed to remain erect. Time passed and Jimmy didn't slow. His mind had evacuated the situation and was sunning itself on a warm beach watching palm trees gently swaying. Alicia's moans and groans peaked several times before Jimmy began to sense something inside him fighting desperately for freedom. It was not what anybody would have expected or wanted. He quickly pulled out, got up and rushed for the bathroom. After five minutes of vomiting every ounce of food and fluid in his stomach and several more minutes of dry wretching, Jimmy washed his face, cleaned his teeth and prepared himself to walk back into the bedroom, hoping beyond hope that Alicia had passed out or fallen asleep from the exertions. Of course Jimmy hadn't taken into account that she had slept on the plane flight and had in fact not moved much during the marathon sexcapade. As he walked into the bedroom and looked down at the bed, he saw Alicia demonstrating her double-jointedness having lifted her legs so that her ankles framed her ears. Looking up at him she whispered, "Now fuck me in the ass, Studly!" It would be wonderful to think that this was a move too far for Jimmy but, and it depends on your viewpoint, he did England proud and satisfied Alicia's every desire until she left the next afternoon, by taxi. A different taxi.

That evening, conversation was at a minimum between the four lads as they sat in the car. Symon was trying really hard not to move as each change in position awoke the pain receptors in his bum and sent slices of agony from each whip cracked welt. Sean sat berating his sensible reaction to his brief encounter. Agreed he was enjoying his freedom but he would have enjoyed it more had he been laid. Was her story really the sign of a psycho? He would never know. Sid's bum was also feeling very tender but for very different reasons and from a far more internal source. His stomach was growling as it got used to surviving on a drastically reduced intake. And Jimmy dared not close his eyes as each time he did a vision of the Michelin man lying on its back with its ankles as earmuffs flashed into his mind. An involuntary shudder and dry wretch accompanied each image. In a desperate attempt to get his mind off recent events, Jimmy asked the lads, "What are we doing at college tomorrow?" Symon, feeling a little woozy, muttered "Lecture Theatre. Welding theory." The other three lads groaned. None of them enjoyed the more academic side of their course but for Symon, who spent most of his day outside in all weathers, the chance to have an hour in the warm was one he cherished.

Ring

Jimmy and Sid sat two rows down from the back with Symon and Sean immediately in front of them. The metalwork class were all there but Terry Wanstrow was rushing round preparing for his next 'Stewartson Suffrage' as he called it. Jimmy wondered why Terry seemed so keen on winding up Mr Stewartson. He couldn't remember any occasions when Stewartson had done anything nasty to Terry. Perhaps Terry just didn't like the Scottish. Whatever the reason, Terry was busy tacking two core wire all around the lecture theatre. He had just sat down when Mr Stewartson strode in. "Hey guys! Let's get our learn on and understand Welding!" To a man the entire class groaned. "Hey now fellas! Welding is cool! Without welding there would be no ships, no cars, no washing machines! Welding literally joins industry together." Again the class groaned. Mr Stewartson turned to the whiteboard, facing away from the class and began to write. A doorbell rang. Mr Stewartson spun round, cocked his head to one side and listened. Hearing nothing more he turned back and continued writing. The doorbell rang again. Mr Stewartson spun round again looking from person to person to see if he could spot the culprit. Seconds passed. He turned back to the board then immediately spun back to face the class, hoping to catch one of them. He saw nothing and turned back. He waited with his hand poised to write. Nothing. He began to write. The doorbell rang. The class began to giggle. Mr Stewartson paused. The doorbell rang. A twitch began to develop on his face. He continued writing. The doorbell rang. Mr Stewartson began mumbling under his breath. The doorbell rang. Mr Stewartson spun round to face the class again. "Which one of you bas ..." he caught himself mid-rant and took a deep breath. Slightly calmed he continued "Hey ..." he forced a chuckle, "... You've had ya laugh, very funny now let's do some learning guys eh?" He turned back to the board, sure he has got through to them. The doorbell rang. He spun back round and threw his pen to the floor. "Right you fuckers! All fucking term you've been riding me and NOW that fucking bell! I'm going to tear it out and ram it down ya fucking throats ya fucking poor excuses for cum stains on ya whore mothers knitted stockings!" His hippy, semi-neutral accent had gone and instead his natural Glaswegian guttural one appeared. He started storming around the lecture theatre looking for the wires. He found one coming from his desk, grabbed it and tore it out. Holding it in the air he laughed maniacally. The doorbell rang. He looked around, confused and angry in equal measure. He started tearing at the wire, following it round the lecture theatre as he went. The doorbell rang again. Desk by desk he pulled the wire from its plastic clips. The doorbell rang. "It's you isn't it Wanstrow?!" He tore more wire away. The doorbell rang. "I'm gonna tear your fucking head off and piss down ya throat THEN shove this fucking doorbell down there for good luck!" The doorbell rang. The class began to edge toward the exit as they witnessed the descent of Mr Stewartson from human to animal. All they could hear was a growling interspersed with some of the foulest language imaginable. The doorbell rang. The class hurried to the exit. "That's it run ya fucking wankers! I'll fucking get ya!" He dropped to his knees as he pulled the end of the wire from a cabinet at the back of the lecture theatre. The class slowly filed out. Mr Stewartson's shoulders bobbed up and down as he sobbed. The last person out of the door was Terry Wanstrow who raised his hand and pressed the button on the remote doorbell ...

Jimmy sat in the car listening to DJ Ed Swarthy, still filling in for the sick DJ, trying to get to grips with modern music that he clearly didn't like. He saw Jennifer walk up to the bus stop. She turned and saw him and with a smile, waved. He smiled and waved back. He was just about to get out and join her when the bus arrived and she got on. He slumped back into his seat. Symon arrived and gently sat down next to Jimmy. "What is wrong with you Slymes? Did you get injured

Bristle

in training?" Symon couldn't look at Jimmy. "Uh yeah. Just bruising. It'll pass." Jimmy didn't believe him but didn't push it. Sean and Sid arrived and hopped into the back seat. "What's with Wanstrow and Stewartson?" Sean asked the lads. "Dunno! He's gonna get us in trouble one of these days!" Sid opined. "I've heard he's got a big one planned for next week. Johnnie Bristow told me." Jimmy added. "How does Johnnie know?" asked Symon. "Dunno." replied Jimmy. DJ Ed Swarthy introduced 'Nutbush City Limits by Ike and Tina Turner'. Sid chuckled. "Have you ever wondered about this song title? Nut? Bush? Hehe." Sean punched Sid on the arm. "Twat!"

The four lads sat in silence through Ike and Tina and then subsequently through Donovan's Season of the Witch. "That reminds me, got any blow?" Sean asked. Symon shook his head. Sid reached into his pocket and pulled out a small baggy and some Rizlas and began to roll a spliff. Sean waited till he was balancing the paper full of marijuana on his lap and nudged his elbow sending it all over his knees. "You wanker!" Sid shouted, gathering the pieces together and starting again. He'd finished rolling it and was in the process of lighting it as DJ Ed Swarthy introduced 'T Rex and their Children of the Revolution'. Taking a big draw he passed the joint to Sean. As Sid exhaled, Sean took a deep drag before passing it forward between the two seats. Symon shook his head so Jimmy took it and drew a deep breath. As Jimmy passed it back to Sid, Symon opened the door. "I've got stuff to do lads. See you tomorrow." Before Jimmy had a chance to say anything, Symon gingerly got out and closed the door behind him. Sid asked "What's up with him?" Jimmy shook his head. "Not sure. He's been that way for a couple of days. Could be his injury. Or it could be cos I had a go at him about not taking his football seriously." The three lads continued smoking until the spliff was all but a scrap of paper. Sid took it and tapped the remainder of dope back into his plastic baggy. DJ Ed Swarthy announced the final song of his set would be 'The Chain by Fleetwood Mac' and the boys sat upright and prepared for the bass guitar riff. None of them could play the bass so they drummed it instead. As they all thought the rest of the song a bit boring, once the bass riff had finished, they all said their goodbyes and left.

Jimmy walked inside his house and went straight to bed. He hadn't been on the virtual world since Alicia had gone home. Out of sight out of mind was his mantra when it came to her. He got undressed down to his boxers and lay on the bed. Thankfully, when his eyes closed, the image he saw was of Jennifer waiting at the bus stop. Wistfully he

Bristle

imagined that her bus was late and that he'd got out of the car and stood with her while she waited. The next few moments were a blur until focus returned with them both lying down on her bed, teddy bears and cushions scattered everywhere. They were naked with her on top of him kissing. He felt her hands move between them. She manoeuvred him into position and sank back onto him. More blurred images. He saw breasts, smiles, glittering eyes but never her whole face. Wonderful sensation upon wonderful sensation filled his mind. The excitement built. He didn't hear his bedroom door open and only vaguely heard a whispered "Jimmy? You there?" as Vickie looked inside. In an immediate shock Jimmy woke up and recognised the moment. Sadly, his body was still dreaming and finished the moment on auto pilot. His stomach flexed and his body jolted as he filled his boxers with spurt after spurt of ... enjoyment. His hands, too late, reached for his groin to cover his embarrassment. Vickie turned bright red and covered her eyes. "Oh I'm so sorry Jimmy! I ... oh my God! I'm sorry!" She rushed out of the room and into her own. Jimmy screamed "Fuck Vix! What the hell ..." He slowly calmed down and laid back on the bed. The silence was broken by the distant sound of a sob. Thinking he had perhaps been a bit over the top in his reaction, he pulled on a T shirt and a pair of track suit bottoms and went to see his sister. He knocked on the door. "Vix? Can I come in?" The sobbing paused. "Um. Sure." came the croaky response. He opened the door slowly and walked inside. "Hey Vix. Sorry I shouted at you. It was ..." Vickie shook her head. "No I'm sorry Jimmy. I didn't mean to ... I just needed to talk." Jimmy moved further inside the room and sat on her bed. "What's the matter Vix?" Jimmy asked. "Man trouble is it?" Vickie looked down at her lap and nodded. "You're having trouble with him aren't you Vix? He's not hitting you is he?" Vickie looked up at Jimmy and paused. "No. He's not." Jimmy was confused. She said no but her actions seemed like she doubted what she was saying. "What's he doing then Vix?" Vickie took a deep breath. "Well ... he ... he's different. In bed. He's ... well he says it's normal but I've never done it before." Jimmy moved closer and put his hand on Vickie's. "You're not talking to Mum or Dad here Vix. You can tell me." She burst into tears. It took her a while to stop sobbing long enough to get her breathing under control enough to talk. "I'm sure I'm just being prudish but ..." Jimmy squeezed her hand. "Well he wants a threesome. I've done the other stuff that he asked but I just feel this is too much." Jimmy's brow crumpled. "Other stuff?" Vickie looked up at her brother. "Well you know ... a bit of experimenting, as he put it, more than just missionary." This conversation was becoming difficult for Jimmy. "Yeah OK Vix.

Difficult for me to comment on that. And as for the threesome, well it IS every red blooded man's dream but that's usually where it stays. My concern is that it always seems to be about what HE wants. He doesn't seem to care about YOUR wishes?" Vickie nodded. "Yes. I'm starting to think that myself. But he's got a good job which Mum keeps telling me is the most important thing. He's quite clever and good looking. And when we first met I really thought this was the one. He was attentive and bought me flowers and stuff." Jimmy nodded. "Does he still buy you flowers?" Vickie shook her head. "I've listened to the stuff Mum and Dad spout just as much as you have and you know I've realised that it's bollocks. THEY never followed any of these 'guidelines' that they put on us! Dad didn't have a good job and though not thick he was no genius." Vickie smiled. "He certainly never bought her flowers!" They laughed. "But you know what Vix? Whenever Mum is sick, he takes the day off work and makes her soup and takes her cups of tea. He doesn't enjoy seaside holidays but they went to Minehead a couple of days ago because he knows SHE likes it. He always takes charge of the washing up on a Sunday afternoon after she's worked all morning on the roastie." Vickie thought for a second. "And Mum suggests he go to the pub after work for a swift one because she knows it helps his mood." Jimmy and Vickie spent a moment in silent reverie. "So the point is perhaps to do as they DO not as they SAY. Find a man who is attentive in the right areas. Flowers matter less than soup when you're ill." Vickie nodded. "I'll give him one more try. I'll talk to him and explain my side of things. Then we'll see where we go from there." Jimmy squeezed her hand again and left her to sleep.

Symon arrived at the big house on the downs and stood by the gates. There must have been a remote camera somewhere as they suddenly swung open. He walked down the long drive and up the stone staircase where he was met by Jenkins. "Mistress is expecting you." Symon had not called ahead so Jenkins' statement was surprising to him. He walked into the large and imposing reception room where Jenkins touched him on the shoulder and led him into a room to the side furnished in Edwardian style with a large roaring fire flanked by two large, comfortable looking chairs. Jenkins proffered one to Symon who sat. "Mistress will be with you shortly." Jenkins quickly disappeared. A few moments later Mistress Donna walked in with Jenkins, holding a tray with glasses on it, in her wake. She sat in the chair opposite Symon and took one of the glasses offered by Jenkins who then offered one to Symon who declined. "So you came back. I thought you would." Fingering a glittering engraved ring between her fingers she continued, "I have your collar." Symon looked seriously at Mistress

Donna. "Yes I did return but perhaps not for the reason you think." Symon looked down at his hands briefly before continuing. "The night we met, you offered me a 'new experience' which you provided. I signed your contract and followed it to the letter of the law even though you did not completely manage your side of the bargain." Mistress Donna looked surprised. "I did not? In what way did I not adhere to my side of the bargain?" Symon winced. "No cuts. No blood drawn. No scars. My ass is proof you failed on that aspect of the bargain. But to a degree it's beside the point. I got my new experience and you got whatever it was you were looking for. I have a feeling that perhaps you got a little carried away at one point which is why I am sat here. You offered ME a new experience and I am grateful. But as sure as I am that you would not be interested in any new experience I could offer you, the role you offered me is not one that I am willing to take. But I wanted to thank you in person and wish you the best in the future." Donna looked somewhat quizzically at Symon. "What made you sign the contract and go through with it? You could have said your safe word at any time." Symon smiled. "You know why and that's why you chose me. All my life I've been told never to quit. The life of a footballer is playing a game as work, to work hard for the applause of the fans and glory of achievement. The effort you put in on the training ground is what enables you to get the most out of the Saturday game. The pain of rehearsal results in the applause of the crowd at the show. But ... the most important lesson that I have learned ... and I have you to thank for that ... is that I love football. I've been *playing* at the game so far in my life and it's time I got serious. So thank you Donna and good luck." Symon stood and moved toward Donna. As she stood, Symon hugged her and whispered in her ear, "Elephant" and turned to walk away. Donna put her hand on his shoulder and stopped him. "Symon, you are right in everything you've said and I am embarrassed that I failed as your Mistress. I let my passion overtake me and that was wrong. But I am glad that you got as much as you did from this experience and I will berate myself forever if I do not also learn from the lesson you have taught me. I know some very powerful and influential people. It's the nature of what I do I suppose. If you EVER need anything, however trivial, just call." Symon nodded but said no more. Jenkins appeared, to open the door and escort Symon from the house.

Jimmy sat quietly in the van having just told Paul all about his conversation with Vickie. Eventually he broke the silence with a question he had long wanted to ask him. "How come I've never seen you with a girlfriend Paul? If you're gay, that's cool. Just wondered." Paul laughed out loud. "Thanks for being OK about that James but no I'm not gay. But my love life is a long story." Jimmy smiled. "Well you're the one who got us a job in Birmingham so time we have." Paul nodded. "My father was what modern medicine now calls bi-polar but within the family was known as the Cavendish Curse. It was a family trait that very occasionally skipped a generation and I thank fate every day that I am in that skipped generation but I can't risk allowing it to pass to the next generation. I'm an only child and if I don't have children then I can ensure the death of the Cavendish Curse. My wife, yes I've been married, had thought she could change my mind and after five years of trying unsuccessfully decided to give up and leave me for my best friend. Five years of arguments and verbal fighting have taken its toll. I haven't dated in the 15 years since the divorce but I do have a long-time relationship with a girl I've known since I was a kid who I gravitate back to from time to time when the hormones need it. I know I love her and always will but fate and my desire to allow her the chance of a good life with someone else always ensured ours would never be more than an occasional tryst." Jimmy sat quietly. "It's strange. My Dad never wanted kids but has two. He's not the worst father in the world but you seem almost designed to be one and yet you, and don't get me wrong – I understand, don't want any." Paul shook his head. "I would love to have kids but I couldn't, I just couldn't curse them with such a tough life." Jimmy pondered for a while. "What about adoption?" Paul smiled. "I have considered that and in truth that would work but something in me has always felt that it made no sense when both parties were capable of having children. I know for a fact that my ex-wife would have resented that forever. But that relationship was always doomed to fail regardless of any issues children brought into it." The conversation was light hearted after that having used up their reserve of seriousness.

Bristle

Carbs

As they arrived outside Jimmy's house, Paul reached under the seat and pulled out a box. Giving it to Jimmy he said, "You've had a tough few weeks and business has been good so here's a small bonus for you." Jimmy looked confused. "Really? Are you sure?" Paul nodded. Jimmy tore open the box and gaped in astonishment. "Wow! Oh Paul! Seriously?" Paul smiled. "Seriously. Now bugger off and let me go to the pub – I need a pint!" Jimmy thanked Paul again and hopped out of the van. He rushed into the house to show the family. "Mum? Dad? Paul got me a brand new carburettor for the car! Mum? Dad?" He stormed into the lounge to find his Mum and Dad lying on top of each other on the floor. The TV blared out sounds of panting and moaning while images of naked people in various positions flickered across the screen. His dad rolled off his mother, ungentlemanly leaving her scrambling to cover her bits. He cupped his manhood with his hands before reaching for his jeans and T shirt. "Um. Hi Jimmy. What's up?" his father asked while pulling on his T shirt and pulling up his boxers. He kicked his legs into his jeans and pulled up the zip. Meanwhile his mum had foregone her bra and slipped her blouse over her head. She too pulled up her panties and struggled into her jeans. They both crawled to and sat on the sofa. "Oh my God! What were you two doing?!" Jimmy shouted. "Oh for Christ's sake Jimmy! Have you never seen two people getting it on?" His mother retorted. "We got needs ..." his father began, "and urges ..." his mother added, "and we're not dead yet son!" Jimmy stood there in shock, shaking his head. "I still needs me some hard cock, Jimmer." his mother said nudging his dad who giggled childishly. "Oh WAY too much information! You couldn't just do it in ya bedroom like normal people?" Thankfully for all the conversation was interrupted by Vickie storming into the house, slamming the door and running upstairs in tears. Jimmy looked at his mum then his dad questioningly who both returned his look with shrugs. Jimmy followed Vickie up the stairs, shouting behind him "This is a conversation we're ..." he thought for a moment, "NEVER going to revisit!". He arrived at the top of the stairs and stood outside Vickie's bedroom. "Vix?" A quiet sobbing was the only reply. "Vix? You OK?" There was a pause followed by "Leave me alone Jimmy!" He waited outside her door for a few moments before replying. "If you want to talk Vix, just shout." He turned and walked into his bedroom. Jimmy sat on the edge of his bed thinking about Vickie. She was probably the most important blood relative to him. Obviously he loved his parents but they were not his peers. Vickie was of a similar age and whatever trials and tribulations had occurred during their lives, they had always been there for one another. Admittedly, sometimes it might have been for a well intended slap but it was equally for a consoling hug. Jimmy felt that Vickie was at a pivotal time in her life and for some reason was careening down the wrong path. He wished he could just take over her decision making process and put her straight but as nobody could do so for him neither could he for her. At that moment the door opened and Vickie peeked around it. "Got a minute Jimmy?" Jimmy looked up at her and simply patted the bed next to him. Vickie sat down and took a deep breath in preparation of spilling the beans. Jimmy put his finger to her lips and whispered "Shhh!" as he pulled her to him and hugged her. She began to cry again and melted into his embrace. He stayed there just allowing her to feel his concern and unload her sadness. Eventually her sobbing subsided and she pulled away from Jimmy a little to look into his eyes. "You always know exactly what to do Jimmy. How do you do that?" Jimmy smiled at her. "I dunno Vix. I guess I just do what I would like someone to do with me. I've not exactly had the experiences you have Vix. I've not been in love or even near it. But when everything is getting me down and I have no clue what to do next, I just want someone to ... well to hug me. I want them to understand that it may not be advice that I need, just empathy." Vix smiled. "Thanks Jimmy." She squeezed him tightly before getting up and returning to her room. Feeling a little better about the situation himself, he laid back on his bed and fell into a light snooze.

Later that evening, Jimmy was sat in the car reading the bumph that had come with his new carburettor. Paul had asked the man at the scrap yard to get him a new one and this one was a high performance four barrel one. Jimmy couldn't have bought one this good if all the lads had saved up for a year! Symon opened the front passenger door and, forgetting his 'issues', plonked down on the seat. "Aghh! Bugger!" Jimmy looked across. "Injury no better Slymes? Are you playing this weekend though?" Symon winced. "No better and no game this weekend." DJ Ed Swarthy introduced 'Mike and the Mechanics – Living Years' just as Sid hopped into the back seat. "Evening Wankahs!" Without the usual gusto, Symon and Jimmy replied, "Spankah." The three lads continued listening to the radio in silence. The back door opened and Sean got in. Now all four lads were present, Jimmy cleared his throat. "I've got some news." Not particularly engaged, the other three lads mumbled words of vague interest. "About the carburettor." All three perked up. Symon asked "Yeah?" Jimmy smiled and passed him the box. Symon opened it and said "Wow! Awesome! Where ... how did you get it?" He passed it to the back seat for Sid and Sean to look. "Paul got it for me. A bonus for working last weekend, well last Saturday." Sean and Sid muttered enthusiastically. "When are you going to fit it?" Symon asked. "Sunday hopefully. I've never done one before and you've got to make loads of adjustments. It might take me a while." Jimmy replied. All three lads nodded. "Awesome." Sean asked "So what's left after that?" Jimmy replied "Wheels, tyres and electrics I guess." The mood in the car visibly lifted. Symon began to shift uncomfortably in his seat. "What the hell's up with you Slymes?" Jimmy asked. With a big sigh Symon replied "It's a long story." He proceeded to finally tell them all about his time with Mistress Donna. "And when I sat in the car tonight, something on my ass burst." Jimmy, Sean and Sid in unison shouted "Ohh gross!" The looks of disgust and nausea remained on the faces of Sean, Sid and Jimmy until Sid asked "Can we see it?" Symon lead the protests but after Jimmy and Sean eventually succumbed to their curiosity he relented, struggled to make space in the front seat for the necessary manoeuvre, dropped his jeans and bent over. His white boxers sported a yellowy-green stain with red and purple hints. Jimmy wretched but Sid said, "Keep going! Lose the boxers!" Symon reached back and pulled down the hem of his boxers revealing a criss-cross pattern of red welts surrounding a swollen lump with clearly broken skin that continued to ooze the vilest looking liquid. Jimmy opened the door and leant out, spewing forth his last meal in copious amounts. Symon pulled up his shorts and jeans and sat back down. Sean took a deep breath. "That's gone septic mate. Seriously septic!" Sid looked shell-shocked. "I've got serious concerns I might get PTSD after that! And you say you've decided not to go see her again? You do surprise me!" The car descended into silence as the four lads tried desperately not to picture the gore they had just witnessed. Known only to one of the occupants an olfactory equivalent to the visual delights of the last few minutes was preparing to announce its presence to the waiting, virginal, unaware nostrils. As with all such moments, the delivery man tried his best to ensure no clue was given or perceived. There was no slight tilt of the body. There was no lifting of the buttock. There was no verbal preparation or siren acting as a three minute warning. There was no countdown. Instead a seeping cloud of pungent poisonous death crept slowly from the cleft crevice that crowned the sewer from whence it had stewed. Like the Master Beer-maker, the owner imperceptibly tested the brew. Noting hints of oats, barley, wheat and rancid milk delicately woven with rotting flesh and pure shit, he smiled to himself and settled back to await the much prized reaction to his efforts.

Sean was the closest to the source but due to the physics of convection currents, Jimmy was actually the first to receive the bounty. In truth his senses overloaded immediately causing his first reaction to actually be the watering of his eyes such as occurs during any moment of potential damage to the membranes. Soon afterwards, as his nose managed to recover, staggering wearily to its feet after the initial knock down blow, it bravely assessed the atmosphere and passed on to the brain a full report. The shock careered across Jimmy's brow causing him to breathe deeply in preparation for a vocal retort to this onslaught. Sadly, his lungs found the atmosphere devoid of oxygen and instead initiated a coughing fit that inadvertently aided the passage of the toxic cloud around the car. Before Jimmy could recover, Sean and Symon joined the audience and having received a slightly watered down version, due to Jimmy's coughing fit mixing the cloud with the available air, were able to respond with such epitaphs as "Fuck me who died!" and "Someone's shit!" followed quickly after with "Sid you wanker!" and "Sid! What crawled up your ass mate?" Meanwhile, Jimmy opened his door and having previously emptied his stomach, dry-vomited for a good 2 minutes. Sean and Symon opened their doors and wafted them like a swan with a broken wing trying to take-off. Sid sat back in his chair and enjoyed both the aroma he had created and the afterglow of damage it caused. This heralded the end of the evening and all four lads left the car, with the windows open, and went their separate ways.

Dogging

As the four lads left college, Sid seemed extra excited. As soon as they were out of earshot from the rest of the class, he outlined his news. "I was on the internet last night just browsing and this window popped up all about dogging." Symon murmured "Popped up did it? All of its own accord was it?" Sid looked annoyed. "Yeah, actually, it did! Anyway, it seems this dogging is all about men and women getting together to shag and stuff. Apparently there's swapping going on and all sorts. The forums were full of middle-aged women going on about how they'd love there to be more young studs at these events cos they get bored of doing the Viagra brigade! So ... what do you reckon?" The other three lads looked at each other and shook their heads. "Oh c'mon! It's been ages since I got a shag and these slappers are gagging for it!" Symon shook his head again. "Exactly! Slappers! Who'd want some rusty old, dry-farting, dusty vag?" Sid looked questioningly back at Symon. "We would! Look, its practice ain't it? Imagine what we could learn from these experienced mature women! Then we go do it to some fit birds our age and BANG! We get a rep for being the best shags in Bristol and we're fighting off the totty like seagulls on chips!" The argument continued for a good twenty minutes until Sid delivered the final blow. "So what else are we gonna do tonight? It's either sit in the car and have another 'evening out' or we go doggin'!" Groans emitted from Symon, Sean and Jimmy in turn followed by a triumphant "Yes!" from Sid. "So where is this dogging event?" asked Symon. "Well there's loads around but I reckon we should steer clear of the one up on the Downs cos that's mainly for ... well Homers. So I reckon we should try Filton Sports Centre. You go over Filton roundabout towards the KFC then hop over the fence and it's in the bushes behind the tennis courts. Nice and private!" Symon laughed. "Doggin? Private? You're havin' a laugh!" They all chuckled at this which helped alleviate the gut wrenching tension they all felt.

The clock slowly ticked to 10 and the four lads took a deep breath and got out of the car to walk the mile from Jimmy's house to the dogging site. As they neared the Filton roundabout, Jimmy began to feel the heightened anxiety that had been milling around him since Sid came up with the idea. "Are we sure about this lads? I mean sex is not exactly a spectator sport!" Sid was ready for this and answered, "What do you mean NOT a spectator sport? The internet was **invented** specifically so that people could watch other people shagging!" Mumbling, Jimmy murmured "Spose so." The shadows of the four lads see-sawed back and forth as they passed under the yellow glow of the street lights. "So what's the plan, Sid?" Symon asked. "Well I'm not exactly sure but I guess we stand around and wait for some horny hotty to come pick us up!" Sid replied. "I'm after a threesome. Two horny hotties for me!" added Sean. This got Symon thinking. "Ere! There's not gonna be any backdoor bangin' is there? No Homers? I can't be doin' with fighting off a bunch of Homers!" As the 'pretty boy' this was a major concern for Symon. Sid placated him. "We'll stick together and keep an eye out. We'll protect **your** backdoor Slymes." They dodged traffic easily as they crossed the dual carriageway opposite KFC and as accomplished urbanites, scaled the fence between them and the sports ground. They made their way slowly through a litter, syringe and condom strewn copse and stepped out into a clearing that looked onto the tennis courts. Like four actors arriving on stage at the beginning of a performance, they stood almost expecting a full audience to greet them with cheers and applause. Instead they found the weirdest kind of nocturnal car boot sale imaginable. Vehicles of varying descriptions, from Ford Kas (must be a bonnet-job, thought Sid) to Transit vans (no doubt kitted out with full double mattress, duvet and Champagne on ice) parked haphazardly up against the metal fencing of the courts. The headlights were on, casting eerie shadows across the grass where people milled around in darkness, lit only from their ankles up. Feeling like they'd arrived at a party in fancy dress, only to find everyone in evening wear, the four lads just stood there watching and trying to understand what was going on. Eventually Sid nudged Sean and said, "Look at that Vauxhall. It's rocking!" Sean followed the direction of Sid's finger and saw the suspension of the car being fully tested laterally. A crowd had formed looking in through the back window. "Come on boys, let's go see what's occurin'." Sid pushed the other three towards the vaunting Vauxhall. They tried to peer in through the back window but the crowd jostled them back so all they witnessed was a couple of bright white orbs thrusting up and down inside the car. They split up and went to both sides of the back doors and peered in. Sean and Jimmy were at the 'head' end while Symon and Sid watched two pairs of tangled shoes. Jimmy and Sean could hear the female participant. "No Dean! I don't want this! Oh my God! People are watching." She looked up and saw faces peering in through the rear window. Then craning her neck she looked above her to the rear door window. She screamed the high pitched scream of shock and embarrassment as she recognised the faces looking down at her. "It's Vickie!" the two faces screamed back in unison. Reaching for the door handle, Sean shouted "I'll fucking kill him!" as Jimmy stepped back to allow the door open shouting "I'll fucking kill **her**!"

Sean grabbed the man's jacket by the shoulders and pulled him straight out of the car. He tried to get up but the trousers and boxers around his ankles prevented it. Sean picked him up onto his feet with the strength of someone used to manual labour all his life and in one movement punched him in the gut. He doubled over in time to meet Sean's upper cut meet his chin and flew backward into Jimmy who was pulling Vickie from the backseat, in a substantially more gentle manner. Jimmy let go of Vickie and turned to face the man who had been thrown at him. Jimmy, when he looked back on the incident, was surprised at how calm and emotionless he was looking at Dean. Without thought or concern for consequences, he punched him in the nose and watched as his nose exploded in a cloud of blood. Dean crumpled to the ground to face a final kick from Sean. Deciding this was not the time to interrogate Vickie, Jimmy grabbed her by the shoulders and firmly told her, "Go home!" Vickie turned and ran with her shoulders moving up and down as the tears flowed. A crowd had formed around the activities but was held at bay by Symon and Sid who, in the best tradition of those that police such crowds, informed the mob to "Stay calm. Family incident. Nothing to see here." The four lads gave each other the universal "Let's get the hell out of here!" signal and began to walk over to the copse. One of the couples that hadn't witnessed the recent goings on, sidled up to the four as they walked away and the middle-aged woman tapped Jimmy on the shoulder. "Going so soon feller? Not up for some fun?" Jimmy turned around and felt all his major organs wither and wilt as he recognised her. "Oh my God, Jimmy! What the hell are you doing here?" Jimmy struggled for breath before replying "Me?! What the hell are YOU doing here, Mum?" He looked across at the man she had in tow. "And Dad!" Before they had a chance to reply, his Dad grabbed his Mum by her arm and dragged her away. Symon, Sean and Sid grabbed Jimmy and walked him out of the clearing, through the trees and home.

Jimmy sat in the van with Paul and realised that he had not spoken a word since he saw his Mum and Dad the night before. Paul had spoken to him several times but the part of his brain that accepted external stimuli had switched off. Eventually Jimmy recovered enough to tell Paul all that he had witnessed the previous night. Paul managed to stop himself from laughing, content in the fact that at some stage Jimmy would come to realise the humour in the situation but that now was not that time. He let Jimmy talk and offered the odd question to coax everything out of his young apprentice. He finally asked if Jimmy had seen Vickie since to which Jimmy answered that he had briefly seen her this morning and noticed she seemed to be wearing more makeup than usual but had not had a chance to talk to her. Paul became both serious and silent at this news. The rest of the day dragged as they both could not, however hard they tried, raise their mood. It was a relief when Paul dropped Jimmy home at a little after 6 that evening.

Bristle

Nuts

"OK so as we've got no parts to buy this week, how about we save our money to have a good night on Saturday?" Jimmy asked the other three lads as they sat in the car that Monday evening. "I'm working on the carb and electrics during the week in the evenings and will be Saturday and Sunday so will need a bloody good sesh ... besides I need new memories, good memories, to block out some of the horror of the last few weeks!" Symon, Sean and Sid all nodded agreement. "So what's ya plan Jimmer? We can't go clubbin' cos its way too expensive and we don't really have any clubbin' gear." Sean asked. "And no ditching when we get there. All together." Begged Sid. "Unless we pull, of course." clarified Symon. "Well I was thinking about perhaps somewhere in Clifton. Nowhere too posh cos we're on a budget but somewhere that would be full of girls." Symon smiled. "And where is this magical place? Does it actually exist or is it just wishful thinking?" Jimmy thought for a second. "Well I reckon if we look on Google Maps for some small pub near the university we could strike gold." Sid scowled. "Nah! That'll be full of student types! Blokes with brains up their noses and girls with sticks up their arses!" Everyone laughed. "Yeah but the nice girls, the ones that we might have a chance with, will be fed up of those pretentious pricks and fancy a bit of straight-forward, down to earth, solid as a

Bristle

rock local types!" replied Jimmy. The four brains generated a shroud of silence as they first assessed the logic of Jimmy's plan and then contemplated the potential outcome. "It's decided then! Southmead goes to Uni!"

The next morning, Jimmy and Paul had a day's work in the Galleries shopping centre in the middle of Bristol. There had been some kind of party overnight that had got out of hand causing quite a few windows to get smashed. "An ill wind" commented Paul. As it neared midday, they were forging ahead making good progress when Paul noticed a few errors on the window signs that had been printed hastily and collected that morning on their way to the shopping centre. He contacted the printing company and explained the mistakes and the urgency. They promised they would be ready in a little over an hour. "Jimmy? I want you to experience a bit more of the managerial side of the business and dealing with suppliers is a very important part. I'm going to stay here and do a bit of prep work and then take lunch. I want you to go to the printers and oversee the job. I want you to see how they do things and get an understanding of their process. It will allow us to perhaps work better with them in the future and might also allow us to find new ways to do business. It also means that they won't slack on the job and you can keep a close eye on them." Jimmy looked concerned. "It's only down the road. You'll be there a couple of hours. Then you can bring back the finished work and meet me here." Even less assuaged by Paul's comments, Jimmy paused. "Oh stop worrying! You'll be fine. You know how to get there from here, by foot?" Jimmy nodded. "Well be off with you then." Jimmy breathed in deeply and puffed out his chest. He turned and strode toward the exit purposefully for about ten steps then looked back at Paul who was watching him. Paul motioned for him to carry on. Jimmy turned and trudged off to the printers. Confident that Jimmy would complete the task and benefit from it, Paul continued to remove the broken pieces of glass from the window and clean out the tracking. After he brushed everything up, he had a word with the store manager who confirmed that they would be open all lunch so he could leave the window unattended, checked the safety barrier and walked towards the far end of the shopping centre. He had been raised to know a soup spoon from a dessert spoon and to discern 'boeuf en croute' from a meat pie but his guilty pleasure and one he succumbed to, with abandon, whenever he was in the Galleries was Burger King. As he neared the door he recognised a very attractive girl walking towards him. It was one of those moments when he knew he knew her somehow but couldn't quite put his finger on why. She happened to look up at him at that precise moment and mirrored his look. Paul rapidly put the pieces together; very attractive, tall, too much makeup, absence of a smile but the kind of face that usually sported one. As they got closer the truth dawned on him. "Vickie?" he asked. She broke into a watery smile. "I'm Paul, Jimmy's boss." Her smile broadened in recognition. "Oh hello, Paul. How are you?" Paul stuck out his hand to shake hers. "Famished! Care to join me for a BK double?" He opened the door and stood waiting for her to enter. This had the desired effect of making up her mind. She passed him saying "I've not got long but perhaps a coffee?" Paul followed her through the door. "Whatever you desire m'lady." Naturally tactile, Paul took her arm and walked with her to the order point. He perused the fluorescently lit menu and as he was asked for his choice, replied, "Bacon Double XL, Double Whopper sandwich, two fries, two onion rings and a vanilla shake." Vickie stuttered a protest. "No Paul I can't. Just a coffee, please." Paul smiled, "and just a coffee for my friend." The kitchen was backed up so the adolescent behind the till suggested they find a seat and they would bring out their order. Paul and Vickie sat at the nearest, sticky though recently wiped, melamine table, sliding over the plastic seats as they did. "So Jimmy tells me you work at John Lewis?" Vickie nodded. "On the perfume counter." Paul smiled as he recollected an item of trivia from his nerdy past. "Do you know the Red Dwarf TV series?" Vickie looked confused at the seemingly untoward jump of conversation but nodded. "Well Lister describes Kristine Kochanski, the love of his life, as so beautiful she could work at the perfume counter of John Lewis's." A slight blush edged through Vickie's makeup and her full smile released its shackles and broke out across her face. Paul smiled again. "And there's her famous pinball smile!" Vickie looked down at her hands. "I'm sorry," said Paul, "I didn't mean to embarrass you. And I'm sure you get told all the time that you are beautiful." Vickie looked up. "Sometimes. Sometimes not enough by the people you want to." This was both a test and an opportunity, Paul realised. How he answered this question would tell Vickie a lot. "Jimmy worries about you, you know? We spend a lot of time on the road and naturally two people get to talking. He's very concerned about your current boyfriend but doesn't really know what role he should take. He wants to protect you even though he is your little brother but also feels that you wouldn't like his interference. He cares about you very deeply you know?" Vickie nodded. The tears began to well behind her lacquered eyelashes. "Well it's over now." Vickie whispered. Paul nodded. "It's a difficult time for you Vickie. You seem to have invested deeply in him, emotionally. And he, as far as I am aware, has thrown away the greatest gift a woman can give a man. People talk of broken hearts and it sounds like a permanent state of affairs but this is only because the heart feels things so strongly. When it does get broken the pain is beyond any other. It's an agony that should never be belittled. But, and I speak as someone who has experienced it, the truth is that it does heal. Your heart is actually a mixture of emotion, memory, hope, expectation and very little rational thought. The process that mends it begins with your mind slowly working through and reliving each memory until they become like the twentieth repeat of a once loved television programme. Only when you become sick of reliving that memory can it be shelved. It works on your hope until you realise that it was a false hope and misplaced. It works on each emotion you felt and turns it to anger for his betrayal before turning them into pity because he was the big loser in all this. And slowly your expectations move from a life with him to a life with someone better. Every lesson learned from love can and should become a light to guide you toward real love." The food arrived and Paul passed Vickie her coffee before taking a big slurp of his Vanilla shake. "I'm sorry Vickie. I didn't mean to preach at you or get all 'worldly wise' on you." Vickie smiled. "It's OK Paul. Jimmy has talked about you a lot too. Much as Dad has always loved us, he's not great at the advice thing. I guess that is why Jimmy and I are so close. We've always leant on each other for support." Paul nodded. "You could do worse. He's very insightful is our Jimmy." Vickie chuckled. "So it's over with Dean? Finito? No doubts?" Vickie looked serious again. "Oh lots of doubts but yes. Over. Finito. It is no more." Paul laughed at the Monty Python reference. "It has ceased to be. Good!" Paul finished off his burgers and was left offering some of his fries to Vickie. She picked the odd one from the carton between sips of her coffee. Throughout the conversation both Paul and Vickie had lost all track of time. Vickie checked her watch. "Oh damn! I'm late!" Paul gently took her wrist and looked at her watch. "Me too! Jimmy will be wondering where I am! I sent him on an errand but he must be back by now." They both got up to leave and Paul shoved the rubbish into the nearest bin before escorting Vickie through the exit. As they stood outside Burger King, they both seemed unable to work out exactly how this chance meeting should end. Eventually Paul thrust out his hand. Vickie took it but rather than shaking it, Paul just held it. "I've really enjoyed spending time with you Vickie. You're a wonderful woman. Please believe you are destined for great things and deserving of the best too." Vickie just smiled and turned away, walking back towards John Lewis's and their perfume counter. Paul stood watching until she turned the corner before waking from his thoughts

Bristle

and rushing back to the broken window. He arrived just a few seconds before Jimmy returned, struggling with a large roll of window decals. "I checked the other signs before they got started on them and found some more errors so we corrected them before they sent them to print." Jimmy reported excitedly to Paul. "Excellent work Jimmy. I knew you were the man for the job." Jimmy noticed a lightness in Paul's mood. "So what did you do for lunch?" Jimmy asked before answering the question himself. "Burger King I bet! And where's mine? I'm bloody famished!" Paul laughed. "Sorry sir, I forgot! We'll grab a takeaway before we leave, deal?" Jimmy smiled and nodded.

The rest of the day went slowly but successfully. They finished all the glass replacements and Jimmy took a bigger role in fixing the window decals. Today might have been a small step in his career, such that it was, but it was one that would lead to bigger steps in the future. They picked up a BK order, Paul's treat, and set off for home. "Just need to swing by Sydenham Garage on the way home. Won't take long." Paul threw into the conversation as they drove out of the car park. Ten minutes later they pulled up outside a gordily beflagged forecourt in front of a hastily erected showroom/office. Paul hopped out of the car and strode purposefully inside. He stood inside the office and looked around. There was one man about 55 years old and three lads in their mid twenties. "Which one of you gentlemen is Dean?" Three of the lads pointed to the fourth and automatically seemed to back away from him slightly. Paul reached across his desk and pulled him out of his chair by his lapels. Lifting him in the air, Paul looked into his eyes and spoke quietly and calmly. "Vickie is now off limits. You are not to contact her by any means. I find out you've spoken to her, texted her, emailed her, looked at her ... you die. Get it?" Dean paused just a little too long, trying to retain some semblance of manliness in front of his co-workers. "YOU GET IT?!" Paul shouted. Dean nodded resignedly. Relaxing his grip a little to allow Deans feet to touch the floor, Paul looked around at the assembled audience. "What do you think the punishment should be for someone who hits women? What do you reckon a BIG MAN like Dean here should get as his reward for hitting a beautiful woman in the face?" The men just shook their heads. Paul looked back to Dean who showed genuine fear in his eyes. He held him at arm's length and with all his force, punched him as hard as he could in the middle of his face, breaking his recently repaired, still plastered nose. He reached up to the earring in his left ear and tugged it out along with a small chunk of flesh. He did the same for his eyebrow ring and nose stud. "For every day you feel this pain just remember this, Deano, this is me calmly enacting some small form of retribution for your bad deeds. You really don't want to meet me when I'm angry, do you?" Eyes weeping from the pain, Dean shook his head. Paul let him go and watched as his body crumpled to the floor. He turned to the older gentleman. "Apologies for the interruption." then turned to the three lads. "Gentlemen." and touched his forehead in a mock salute before turning and walking out of the office. He walked a little slower back to the van and hopped in. "Thanks for waiting James." Paul drove the rest of the way one-handed so that he could hide the abrasions on his right hand and because it hurt like hell when he tried to grip the wheel. He dropped Jimmy off at his home before driving on to his local pub where he quickly swallowed a couple of Rum & Cokes and two painkillers. The rest of the evening blurred a little.

Saturday evening came round all too quickly and Jimmy sat in the car in a better mood than he had been for a long time. It looked like Vickie had finally kicked Dean into touch and had been out on a date the night before and returned from it in a really good mood. Work was going well. Paul had given him more and more responsibility, even leaving him to work alone for long periods when they were working in the city centre. "Probably succumbing to his Burger King fetish."

Jimmy mused. The car was coming along nicely. Most of the electrical problems were fixed and he felt positive that he would have the new carburettor fully installed by the end of Sunday. He was in the best 'gear' he owned and for some reason felt full of confidence about their plans for the evening. Sid hopped into the back seat in an equally good mood which seemed in stark comparison to Sean's when he arrived. Jimmy and Sid couldn't, however hard they tried, get out of him what was ailing him. Eventually they gave up in the hope that a few beers might loosen his tongue. Symon arrived and nearly shouted "All's good for town and beer and birds and ..." he looked confused and already partially drunk. Jimmy, Sean and Sid figured he'd perhaps had a tipple for Dutch courage on his way or maybe celebrated too much after his game earlier that day. Jimmy made the universal 'keep an eye on him' signal towards Sean and Sid who nodded in understanding and agreement. Once they were all together, Jimmy sprung a surprise. "As a small celebration of a good week and a good plan, I've got us a taxi. We'll have to walk home but at least we'll arrive there in style." Sean and Sid whooped with glee while Symon just smiled a little harder. Sean had been out hunting all day with his father so was not looking forward to a long walk into Clifton and Sid was just not a fan of any exercise. A few minutes of chat later, the taxi pulled up in front of the house. The four lads got out of their car and into the taxi for the ten minute drive to the hopefully student-filled pub that Jimmy had googled. The four lads stood on the busy street looking up at neon flashing signs advertising music, games and the name of the theme pub 'Bitter and Twists'. Symon, Sean and Sid looked at Jimmy with incredulity etched across their faces. "Really? This is the place you researched and picked out?" Sid asked. Jimmy smiled and shook his head. "Follow me lads." He turned and walked down a side street. A hundred yards down the road they found a small frontage with frosted windows, peeling green gloss panelling and a tiny door. The sign swinging above the entrance read 'Wag & Hors' because the rest of the letters had worn away. Jimmy pushed inside followed by Symon, Sean and Sid. The sight that met their eyes could not have been more perfect. The place was heaving with small cliques and gaggles of student types sipping halves of beer and lager while talking loudly and passionately with flailing hands and wild gestures. Jimmy made for the bar and whispering to the three other lads "When in Rome", turned to the barmaid and asked for four halves of beer. She smiled a lukewarm smile and poured their drinks before, with outstretched hand, asked for eight quid. Jimmy handed her a tenner and awaited his change. Meanwhile the other three took their drinks and turned to face the rest of the pub like a cheetah looking across the plain. Symon staggered a little as he took a sip of his beer but caught himself against the bar. Sean gazed around with lifeless eyes like his heart just really wasn't in it but Sid's eyes glittered with enthusiasm and excitement. Jimmy too seemed excited with this plan and keen to engage with the student-types. The next ten minutes were spent with Jimmy and Sid trying to make eye contact while Sean and Symon just leant against the bar looking uninterested. This might normally have been the best approach but on closer inspection Symon looked like he was already drunk and another half from collapsing into a drunken stupor while Sean sported a grimace that coupled with his disinterest put off any potential interest. Having emptied their halves, Sid passed Jimmy a twenty and said "Get pints this time!" Jimmy turned to the bar and found the barmaid wiping glasses immediately behind him. Jimmy smiled at her and asked for "Four pints of beer please." She took the empties from him and put them in a plastic tray for washing before grabbing four pint glasses from underneath the counter. As she poured the beers, Jimmy looked at her, properly, for the first time since they had arrived. She was attractive in a not trying to be kind of way. She wore no makeup and dressed in her uniform with a casual elegance that Jimmy liked. Her auburn hair was tied in a bunch and the pony tail flitted around her shoulders as she turned. Jimmy wondered if previous boyfriends had died from whiplash. Deciding honesty was the best approach he asked her, as she placed the four full pint glasses on the bar, "I bet you see this kind of thing all the time eh?" She looked quizzically at him so he continued. "Irregulars coming to try and chat up the regulars." She smiled. "Not exactly subtle are we? We're all from Southmead and ... well ... this was my dumb idea!" She broke into a chuckle at his honesty. "I'm Jimmy ... but if you like you can call me James." He threw her a wink with his introduction. "Pleased to meet you ... Jimmy." She shook his outstretched hand. "And your name is?" he asked. "Confidential ... until I decide otherwise." Jimmy laughed. "Fair enough. Well it's nice to meet you, confidential." Sid got bored of waiting for his pint so reached past Jimmy and passed one to Sean and one to Symon. A tall girl with a slightly ruddy complexion had been sitting near the window chatting with a group of students. She had purposely sat in the corner so that if and when the conversation bored her, she could participate in her favourite activity of people watching. The conversation had turned to Asian politics which was a particular pet hate of hers and so she had begun to look around the pub. Her initial scan was to identify the different groups. As she looked from left to right she checked them off. "Art students, Science geeks, Philosophy, Psychology and ... hmmm ... tough one ... oh I have it ... medical." Before she had time to hone in and analyse each individually a new group arrived. Four young lads that clearly didn't fit with the usual clientele that frequented the 'Wag & Hors' came striding in with a purpose to their step. She put her analytical processes to work immediately, starting with Sean and never got the chance to look further. She saw in him someone who had the weight of the world on his shoulders, who lived a principally outdoor life, who was unsure of his future and was currently tangling with a moral dilemma. She picked up her glass and without saying a word to her friends, squeezed between their chairs and made a beeline for Sean. "Hi. I'm Jo." Sean, who had been staring into the distance and hadn't noticed her arrival, focused on her face and smiled. "Hello Jo. I'm Sean." He looked over her face. She had beautiful lips, sparkling eyes and straw coloured hair. He could tell by the quickening of his heartbeat that he was immediately smitten. "I see great sadness in you, Sean. I'm no seer but I do have a sixth sense for these things." Sean looked at her seriously. "I'm not sure I know you well enough to go bearing my heart." Jo smiled. "Or, perhaps because I am a perfect stranger, there's no danger. You may never see me again in the rest of your life so what's the harm?" Sean smiled lightly. "You make a good point, Jo." He paused before leading her to a quiet corner of the pub. "It's nothing major really. It's just something that has been playing on my mind ever since I started hunting with my Dad when I was ten. He bought me a second hand shotgun for my birthday, took me out and taught me how to hunt. Back then it was easier to deal with the thought of killing wild, free creatures because we were very hard up and ate everything we shot. Rabbit pie, Woodpigeon ... they were all for the table. But as time went on and we started shooting crows because they ate the corn we planted, rats and squirrels because they were vermin etc etc, I found it harder and harder to deal with it. It was one thing to go out hunting with a purpose and to shoot only what we needed for survival but totally another to shoot as many of a certain creature as we could find. Well today came another lesson. My father shot a rabbit and for the first time I'd ever witnessed, he only winged it. The poor thing was squealing in pain and Dad told me to 'dispatch' it. He told me it would be a good lesson in doing the 'right thing', the 'humane' thing. I must admit my immediate reaction was to wonder if the 'right thing' was for him to do it as he had winged it. But I went up to the rabbit and caught it in my hands and quickly, as I had been taught, I snapped its neck. Its suffering was over. Dad then told me to leave it there for nature to deal with as it was too small to bother with and we had a full freezer. As we walked back to the farm, I relived the warmth of the animal between my hands and the noise and feeling as I snapped its neck. I felt the blood trickle across my fingers and absent-mindedly wrung my hands like Lady Macbeth. When we got home, having walked the whole way in silence, I took my gun apart, cleaned it thoroughly and put it away, for the last time. So there you have it. That's what is on my mind." Jo took a deep breath, leaned forward and kissed Sean on the lips before hugging him closely.

Jimmy was leaning over the bar chatting to the ginger barmaid when Sid tapped him on the shoulder. Not wishing to break the spell of talking to this pretty girl, Jimmy tried to ignore him. Sid tapped his shoulder again. "Get some peanuts, mate." Jimmy continued talking to 'confidential'. Sid prodded him harder. "Peanuts. I'm starving!" Jimmy sipped his pint. "Nuts! Get some nuts Jimmer!" Jimmy swivelled and turned to Sid. "Oh for fuck's sake it's like having a kid! Alright! I'll get you some nuts if you'll just shut the fuck up!" Sid nodded and smiled. Jimmy turned back to the barmaid and asked, "Can I have a bag of nuts for the little boy please?" She smiled and asked, "Salted,

Bristle

Dry Roasted or Cashew?" Not sure which, Jimmy decided, "Let's go for Cashew ... push the boat out on this special occasion!" She smiled and grabbed a bag of cashew nuts from the counter behind her. Jimmy passed them back to Sid without looking. Sid tore the bag open and poured the entire contents into his mouth. The barmaid moved to the far end of the bar to serve some other customers and Jimmy just gazed after her. He took a couple of large gulps from his pint in time to witness the barmaid returning. "So how many nights do you work here?" She began to slice a lemon. "Wednesday to Sunday nights and weekend lunchtimes. I don't work Monday or Tuesday nights." Sid prodded Jimmy's back again. "So if a fella was to ask you out then a Monday or Tuesday night would be a good one to pick?" She smiled and nodded. "And what sort of thing would such a fella suggest to do on such a date?" She shook her head. "No clues." Sid clawed at Jimmy's back. "I'm guessing that someone who works in a pub probably wouldn't want to go out for a drink on her night off?" Sid pressed against Jimmy and grabbed his shoulder. The barmaid motioned toward Jimmy with a movement of her head. Jimmy turned round and shouted "For fuck's sake Sid! I'm talking here." Automatically he turned back to find the barmaid had disappeared. In the time it took him to realise, he suddenly put together all the actions from Sid over the last couple of minutes and turned back in time to catch Sid as he slowly crumbled to the floor clutching his throat and turning deep purple. The barmaid was immediately by his side. She had her phone in her hand and was talking into it. "Wagon & Horses, South Parade, Clifton. Anaphylaxis. Hurry!" She hung up and shouted to the bar, "Anybody got antihistamines?" One of the students from the bunch Jo had previously recognised as medical rushed over. "I've not got anthistamines but I've got an EpiPen for my own allergy." The barmaid reached out and took it from the guy. She flipped the top off and slammed it into Sid's thigh and held it there for a couple of seconds before removing it. She supported Sid's head and kept checking his breathing. In no time two quick response paramedics arrived. The barmaid passed one of them empty EpiPen and explained what had happened and that Sid never stopped breathing or lost consciousness but was otherwise quite unresponsive. They hooked Sid up to a number of devices and helped him into a wheelchair. They took him out to their car and Jimmy helped them get him into it. One of the paramedics got in with Sid while the other told Jimmy to get in the front. Sean and Jo were stood outside. Sean tapped Jimmy on the shoulder and said, "We'll meet you there." Jimmy nodded, quickly got in the car and buckled up as they sped off with sirens wailing and lights

Bristle

flashing. In less than five minutes they pulled into the accident and emergency car park where they were met by a team of nurses and doctors with a stretcher who took Sid out of the car and lay him on the stretcher. Jimmy got out and watched as a blur of people and unfamiliar words bombarded his senses. He thanked the paramedics, shaking their hands like a new father and followed Sid inside. One of the nurses took him to one side and walked him to the waiting area. She spoke quietly to him. "Your friend will be fine. As soon as we hear anything we will let you know. Do you want to inform his parents?" Jimmy nodded. He quickly phoned Sid's home and spoke to his Dad. "Hi John, its Jimmy. Sid's had a reaction to some nuts. He's at BRI A&E. They say he'll be fine but we've only just got here. Yes I'm here. Course. See you and Joan soon" He hung up. He found he couldn't sit down being full of nervous energy so he stood up and started pacing. He watched as drunks and young fighters came in expecting immediate service while giving nothing but grief to the staff. He felt the anger growing inside him. One particular drunk lad with a broken nose and a swollen jaw was shouting at the nurse behind the reception desk. Jimmy was just about to go over and put him down when Sean and Jo arrived either side of Symon who they half carried. They'd not long said their 'hellos' and Jimmy had caught them up with the little he knew when Sid's parents, John and Joan, arrived before Jimmy had chance to ask about Symon. Jimmy suggested John and Joan let the reception nurse know they had arrived. She might tell them more than she had him. They walked over to her and briefly waited patiently behind the bruised inebriate that had angered Jimmy so much. John was a smidge over seven foot tall and a good 30 stone so when he tapped the drunk on the shoulder to ask him politely to get out of the way and go sit quietly like a good little boy, it looked like Hagrid talking to a first year Harry Potter and the drunk meekly obliged. Jimmy turned to Sean and Jo. "What's up with Symon? Did he get on the shorts or something?" Sean shook his head. "I don't think so. He barely touched the pint Sid bought him so as far as I know all he's had is a half." Jimmy murmured in confusion. John and Joan returned. "No news but they reckon that because he was given something for it at the pub that he'll be fine. Apparently the barmaid did a great job or so the paramedics said." Jimmy smiled. John looked at Symon. "Has he drunk much?" Sean and Jimmy shook their heads. "Hardly anything." John turned to the Nurse. "Can you get a Doctor out here please? I think this lad has concussion." The Nurse disappeared through the double doors behind her and returned with a white coated female Doctor in tow.

Bristle

They came over to where Sean and Jo and seated Symon. The Doctor knelt down and examined Symon. She turned to John and said, "Good catch." Turning to the Nurse she said, "Get a gurney in here." The nurse rushed off and returned with another nurse and a stretcher. Everyone helped getting Symon on it before he was wheeled away. John turned to Jimmy and said, "Eventful night! Are you OK to call his parents?" Jimmy nodded saying, "His family is in Wales but I've got the number of his coach at Rovers." Jimmy dialled the number and woke the slumbering ex-pro. He talked to him for a while before hanging up. "He'll be here later. Says he was involved in a collision during the game today but seemed fine. Must have been a delayed reaction." Jimmy, Sean, Jo, John and Joan sat in the waiting area awaiting news. Jimmy was watching the double doors, anxious for news on Sid and Symon. After an hour and a half of waiting, he was about to find someone to ask, having pestered the rest of the waiting group enough with his exasperated "Where is everyone? Are they doing anything?" the double doors opened and two nurses came in and walked straight towards them. Jimmy stood up. A confused wrinkle stampeded across his forehead as he recognised the ginger haired nurse. She came up to him as everyone else stood up and crowded round. "Hi Jimmy. Firstly, Sid is fine. He had a very bad reaction to the cashew nuts but he's sat up in bed and chatting the rear end off anyone willing to listen." She looked conspiratorially to her fellow nurse who just smiled demurely. "We'll be keeping him in overnight but only as a precaution. He'll need to get tested for this allergy but there's no damage or long term issues." John and Joan sighed in relief. "Now Symon had a delayed reaction to a concussion he received earlier today. He will be going for an MRI scan shortly and no more can be said until the specialist has gone over it. But he too is sat up in bed and is fully aware of his surroundings. After his scan you can go in to see him but for now you need to just wait. The Doctor on call will be out in a minute to go over this all in greater detail but she let me pop out now and at least give you some information." Everyone relaxed and individually realised that they had tensed up while listening to the nurse. Their shoulders eased and their breathing returned to normal. The ginger haired nurse took Jimmy to one side as the other nurse returned through the double doors. "You never mentioned your 'proper' job." Jimmy smiled as he spoke to her. "Well we hadn't got round to it and I don't tell everybody." She replied. "So I can come in and see Sid in a bit? After his parents of course." "Actually he has asked to see you now. For some reason he said his parents can wait. I'm to take you through now." Jimmy looked a little surprised but followed her through the double doors. Jimmy put his hand on her shoulder to stop her before they reached Sid. "Before I see him, I just wanted to say thanks for what you did at the pub. Clearly you saved his life and ... well it means a lot." She looked at Jimmy. Her eyes stared into his. "Well I didn't want our first meeting to end badly in case you didn't ask me out on that date!" Her face didn't even show a sign of humour. Jimmy loved that. She passed him a note and said simply, "Call me." and turned to continue towards Sid. Jimmy called after her as he run to keep up, "Call me what?" She turned back to him and was tempted to say "Please" or "Anytime" but instead said "Call me Ally." She ushered him through the curtains surrounding Sid's bed and left him there. Sid looked up at Jimmy and smiled broadly. "Best night EVER!" He laughed. Jimmy sat next to him on the faux leather chair provided. "You enjoyed it eh? You like nearly dying huh?" Sid laughed. "I don't think it was quite that bad but the important thing is ... got a number!" Jimmy looked confused. "Waiting list for God or something? Long queue is it?" Sid chuckled. "No you tit! Got the number of a cute nurse. Not your ginger one, the other one." Jimmy shook his head. "You numpty. But fair play. Not many could turn a trip to hospital into a night on the pull! Congrats! Look, your Mum and Dad are here and beside themselves. You can tell me all about it tomorrow when we get you home, ok?" Sid nodded. Jimmy stood up and gave him a playful punch on the arm before battling with the curtains to find the way out. He saw Ally stood by the Nurses station and in a whisper with sign language attached he asked which cubicle was Symon's. Ally pointed to the one next to Sid's. Jimmy gesticulated "Two seconds" mouthing the words as he did so. Ally smiled and nodded. Jimmy poked his head through the curtains and saw Symon laying semi-upright in bed. "Alright dickhead?" Symon looked up at him and smiled. "I can't stop but I'll be in later for a chat, ok?" Symon went to nod but immediately thought better of it and just put his thumbs up. Jimmy pulled his head out of the curtains and walked over to Ally. He held out his palm and pretended to tap numbers in it while reading the note. He held his palm to his ear and made a ringing noise with his lips. Ally laughed but played along. She acted as if her phone was ringing and patted her pockets. She pulled out her flat palm and looked at it, pressed it with her finger and held it up to her ear. "Ahoy, hoy?" Jimmy smiled. "Hi Ally, this is Jimmy. I wondered if you fancied going bowling on Monday evening, say 7ish?" Ally smiled. "That sounds fun. Pick me up at my flat. It's the one to the left of the 'Wag and Hors', top bell." Jimmy chuckled. "Great, see you then." He tapped the middle of his palm and put it in his pocket, smiled at Ally and walked out through the double doors. As Jimmy came back into the waiting area he beckoned John and Joan and said "You can go and see him now." John patted him on the shoulder as he and Joan walked through the doors. Jimmy saw a short, bow-legged man with a slight belly on him dressed in a dark blue tracksuit walk inside looking around. He had the initials DS on the breast and right thigh. Jimmy walked over to him and said, "You must be Donnie, Symon's coach?" The small man smiled and in a broad Scottish accent replied, "Aye, son. Who are you?" Jimmy shook his hand. "I'm his mate, Jimmy. We've just been told that he's ok and sat up in bed. They're doing an MRI soon and more tests tomorrow but a Doctor will come out soon and tell us everything." Donnie kept shaking Jimmy's hand, "Ah thanks, son. That's great news. You're a good pal to him." Jimmy led Donnie over to the rest of the group and made the introductions. They all stayed there for the rest of the night, snoozing occasionally and uncomfortably until morning. Donnie had popped out to the nearest McDonalds and returned with breakfast meals and coffee for everyone. They'd just finished when the Doctor came out and greeted them all. "Firstly, Sid, he's right as rain and ready to go home. He has appointments next week to see a specialist about his allergy and your GP will take it from there." Looking straight at Donnie he continued, "Now, Symon. His reaction was a delayed one to a concussion he experienced during the game on Saturday afternoon and in truth this is very rare and not much can be done to stop such things happening again. The MRI has come back completely clean but I want him to see a specialist before he plays again. He's booked in for a week Thursday so no training other than fitness until then, ok?" Donnie nodded. "Aye, you're the boss. So no indication that it could end his career?" The doctor nodded. "None at all so far but the final decision on that will be made by the specialist." Donnie shook the doctors hand furiously and thanked her profusely before the doctor turned and left. Donnie, for some reason, started shaking everyone's hands like a proud new father and handing out tickets to the next Rovers home game. "I'll take the wee lad home and I'll see you all soon!" He waddled through the doors to get Symon. John looked at Jimmy and Sean and said, "Do you two want a lift back with us?" Sean looked at Jo and said, "Thanks but we're going to spend the day together. I'll find my own way home." Jimmy looked up and said, "Yes please." Sean and Jo walked through with them to Sid's bed where he was sat fully clothed and ready to go. They spoke briefly with him before leaving. Jimmy followed behind John, Joan and Sid to the car park.

Bristle

Premature Matriculation

Tuesday morning came and Jimmy stood with Sean leaning up against the wall of the metalwork room. They were both surprised to see Sid coming from one direction and Symon from the other. For once, Symon was not in his usual uniform of tracksuit and trainers. Jimmy said, "I didn't expect to see you two for a week! Bit keen aren't ya?" Sid spoke, "I had to get out of the house! Mum was all over me. I'm sick of soup and chocolate biscuits that I had to throw out of the window cos I'm dieting!" Symon laughed, "I WISH I was getting that treatment! I'm sat on my ass all day watching Swollen Women or something! Needed to get some reality!" At that moment Terry came round the corner. "Hey lads! 'Stewartson Suffrage' Part III today ... just go with it." The rest of the group turned up in ones and twos until they formed a small crowd outside the room. Mr Stewartson arrived and let them all in. He stood at the front shuffling through his papers while everyone took their usual seats. The murmur of young lads chatting created the typical background buzz. Terry Swanson was sat at the back with his best mate Jack. Terry gave him the nod and their pre-arranged dramatisation began. Jack started shouting at Terry. "What the fuck has it got to do with you? I can shag who I like!" Terry played the part like a pro. "She's my Mum! You can't shag a blokes Mum! That's out of fucking order!" Jack stood up. "Oh fucking get a life! It's not like I'm the only one round here who's shagged her! She might as well park round the back of B block with the other BIKES!" Terry stood up too at this point and pushed Jack who stumbled backwards into the wall. Mr Stewartson was interrupted by the ruckus at this stage and walked towards the two lads trying in vain to calm them down. "Hey guys! Calm down. No need for violence!" Terry turned to see Mr Stewartson coming towards him and grabbed Jack. He turned to face the teacher with Jack in front of him in an arm lock around his throat. Terry pulled a gun from his jacket pocket and aimed it at Jack's head. Unbeknown to Mr Stewartson it was a starter pistol Terry had found in his Dad's shed. They'd tested it during one of their 'rehearsals'. Mr Stewartson turned white. "Now Terry! Put that down! Don't ruin your life lad! This can all be sorted out!" Terry looked daggers at Mr Stewartson. "Oh yeah right! You bastard! You've had it in for me from the beginning! You can't trust anyone! 'Specially teachers!" Terry looked down at Jack and screamed, "Fucking bastards all shagging my Mum!" He began to sob quite convincingly. He paused and looked up at Mr Stewartson. "I bet you've been shagging her too! Haven't you?!" He turned the gun on the teacher who froze like a statue. Stuttering wildly, Mr Stewartson managed to get out, "No Terry! Of course not!" Terry looked angrier. "Ya too good for my Mum are you?!" Jack took this chance to wriggle away from Terry and jump in front of Mr Stewartson. "I'll save you sir!" he shouted. Terry fired the starter pistol four times in rapid succession. Jack twitched his body at each report, clutched his chest (while actually bursting a balloon full of pig's blood) and like the Oscar winner this performance merited he fell to the ground gasping for breath. Mr Stewartson dropped to his knees and held Jack's head in his hands. "Jack! Jack!" Terry kept the gun pointing at Mr Stewartson. "You bastard Stewartson! You made me kill my best friend!" Stewartson looked up with pitiful eyes. "But he was shagging your Mum!" he whimpered. Terry fired again and again. Stewartson clutched his chest and fell backward but not in an Oscar winning performance, more in a 'major heart attack' reaction. There was no riotous laughter. There was no curtain call. There was no applause. Instead there was a call to the Emergency services and the arrival of an ambulance. The head of the college was called and the lads were marched to wait in the corridor outside his office while he interviewed them all. Everyone relayed the same tale. Some included the doorbell incident and others the golden shower. Terry and Jack had been the first into the office and to their favour they didn't shy from the responsibility, admitting their part in everything. They were immediately expelled. Jimmy, Sean, Symon and Sid were the last group to see the head. They already knew that the others had named names and explained everything so there was no harm or honour in holding anything back. The head listened quietly until they all had their say. "You four have been part of a class that may well have killed a man and certainly, minimally, ended his career. At no point did you come to me or anyone here or even your parents and express concern at Terry's treatment of Mr Stewartson. This is a lesson for life boys. If you don't stand up and do what's right when it matters then you face punishment like the cowards you are. You are all excluded from college until further notice. This will go on your permanent records. I want to see each of you one week before the beginning of next year at which time you will tell me if you have decided to grow up and learn at this establishment or if the college would be better without you. Take this time boys and use it wisely. Maturity is a state of mind mostly, and it's time you decided what state your mind is in. Now get out." He spun his chair around and looked out of his window. The four lads trudged slowly out of his office. Symon was the first to speak as they walked out of the building. "That's my apprenticeship over! Rovers will kick me out for this!" Sean spoke next. "That's decided my life that has. No choices now. I'll be a farmer

and I hate farming!" Sid and Jimmy in unison said, "My parents are gonna kill me."
The next evening the four lads were sat in the car. None of them had spoken. It was as if they were waiting for them all to be present before they revealed the extent of their punishments. Jimmy spoke first. "I told Paul. He didn't shout or show any anger at all. That was what was worst. He just went quiet. We did some jobs in Swindon and he didn't speak at all. He waited until we got back here before he said anything. He told me to take a couple of weeks 'garden leave' and think things through. If, after that, I wanted to come back and work for him properly with a desire to actually make a career then he would consider it but otherwise it was over. He was so disappointed in me! I hated making him feel that." Sid nodded. "That's what I got from my parents. I thought I might get away with some post 'allergy' sympathy but there was none of it. They told me that I either sort myself out and work hard in college or I get a job. Two choices." Sean spoke next. "I got the full treatment from my Dad. Mum didn't speak at all but didn't really have to. Dad said I was a dickhead because college was my only option. The farm wouldn't last a year so even following in his footsteps was not an option. They're planning to sell the farm next year after they do some work turning it into a large house with small cottages where the

outbuildings and sheds are and selling off the land for development. He didn't give me a choice because he couldn't think of one." Symon spoke last. "Coach came to see me at the digs. I've been released by Rovers. I've got two weeks to get out of the digs." Jimmy looked shocked. "Where do you go after that?" Symon shrugged. "Home. Or find another club. Not sure anyone else will take me after this and the concussion thing." A fog of silent depression filled the car. The clock ticked loudly against the background of the strange electrical buzz that always accompanied it. As if attempting to wipe away the heavy fog, the windscreen wipers, that Jimmy had thought he had fixed, decided to go into fast mode and whipped across the screen several times before whining to a vertical stop. This seemed to shake Jimmy from his reverie. "Right! There's only one solution! We need to get away. We all have stuff to think through and we can't do it here. Sid looked up. "You mean ... ROAD TRIP!?" Jimmy turned in his seat and looked back at Sid. "That's exactly what I mean!" Symon looked at Jimmy. "Can't do any harm. I've got nothing else to do." Sean was the only one looking unsure. "Can you really imagine me saying to my Dad, 'I'm going off for a lads trip'? He'll throw a fit!" Jimmy smiled. "I've thought about that. You need a strategic *pity plan* that will lay the groundwork for getting the right result. Start by going to see him. Ask him if you could have a word with him. Make it a serious, private, Father and Son chat. Tell him you've taken on board everything that he has said and that you will put all your efforts towards sorting yourself out and growing up. Say you've been in a rut lately and lost your way a little. Leave it at that but go and see him again a couple of days later and suggest that you need to get away to think things through. Tell him that being around the farm, knowing of its impending demise, is not helping. Don't tell him about our trip then, just say you're thinking about the best way to move forward. Then finally ask him if he thinks that perhaps a week ... Bugger! Just thought! Where are we going to go?" Sid laughed. "Already sorted bud. Nookie!" Jimmy looked confused. "Nookie?" Sid replied, "Yeah ... Nookie ... in Cornwall! Surf, sea and shaggin'" Jimmy laughed. "Newquay! Yeah good idea. What do we reckon?" He looked to Symon who shrugged. "Sure, whatever." Sean nodded with a smile. "But with the following proviso – we each get five vetoes to use whenever someone suggests an activity we don't want to do. No arguing over them – veto means no go. Deal?" The other three lads nodded and Jimmy continued his plan. "So you ask him if he thinks that perhaps a week on the coast might help. Somewhere very different to here. Somewhere that you can spend time with your thoughts. Worth a go?" Sean shrugged.

"I'll try." Sid chuckled. "Awesome! Road Trip!"

The Journey Begins

Jimmy redoubled his efforts to get the car finished and by Friday he had started the engine for the first time since they bought it and was happy with how it sounded. Over the weekend he fitted the wheels with the new tyres they had previously saved up and paid for but left with the tyre place. All four of them were present when they lifted it up on the front jacks and removed the bricks. It looked especially racy while still up on bricks at the rear but still looked good after they removed those too. All four lads got in for the inaugural trip round the block. Jimmy started the engine and slowly set off. The steering was a little spongy at first, as were the brakes which barely worked the first time he pressed them but as the fluids got used to their role everything started to become more responsive. Three turns later and Jimmy parked it in front of the house on the road for the first time and the other three lads cheered while Jimmy breathed a huge sigh of relief. That evening Jimmy bled the brakes and steering system and went to bed, for the first time, feeling that the car was finished. Of course he slept less than an hour as every sound outside made him jump up and go to the window to check some thieving bastard wasn't nicking his car! The plan had worked with Sean's Dad and the trip was planned. They would set off early Monday morning and would take the back roads rather than

Bristle

the motorway because Jimmy was not 100% sure that the car could cope with going at over seventy miles per hour. Jimmy had spent a couple of dates with Ally and had nearly forgotten entirely about Jennifer. Sid was talking and texting with his nurse quite a bit and Sean was quite infatuated with Jo. Only Symon was truly single, having ended his relationship with Donna the Dominatrix a few weeks before. Any lesions on his heart had healed along with those on his ass.

Jimmy was up with the sun, one backpack full as agreed, and checking fluid levels and air pressures. He'd cleaned and polished the car the day before but was giving it a final buff as the rest of the lads arrived. They threw their bags in with Jimmy's in the boot and got into their usual seats. It had been decided by drawing lots on the day they had the car delivered to Jimmy's front garden and they had stuck with it without complaint. Jimmy gave Symon a map and instructions that he'd printed off Google and started the car. It purred into life and off they went. It was still early so the traffic wasn't too bad but neither were the roads empty. They headed towards the M32 and the ring road that would take them along the outskirts of Kingswood, Hanham and on to Keynsham where a little bit of almost off-roading would get them onto the A37 heading south. The instructions for getting through Keynsham and via the back roads to the A37 were very complicated and several times they felt lost but stuck with it and after pausing for a moment in Publow by an oxbow in the river to check that they had followed the route as Google had planned. They had, so continued until they met the A37 at Pensford. Everyone relaxed for the next few miles after they had successfully got out of Bristol without meeting major traffic. The usual banter batted around the car and for all their issues, their mood was light. As they neared Clutton, Symon suggested they go off the planned route and through Wells as he had always wanted to see the Cathedral. Jimmy joined the groans from Sean and Sid reminding Symon that this was a boys week in Newquay not a school trip so they stuck to the plan and stayed on the A37 towards Shepton Mallet. The plan didn't last much longer because as soon as Sid saw a sign to Glastonbury, the spiritual home of weed smoking and all things hippyesque, he began to whinge like a small child that they couldn't be so close to Weed Town and not go visit it. Sid also mentioned that they could go see the Glastonbury Festival site that they had always planned to go to but never had the money. Symon and Sean both agreed with Sid so Jimmy felt forced into going with the flow and leaving the plan, at least for the time being. So they took the turn to Glastonbury and drove through the sleepy village of Pilton, not realising that they had passed the home of the Glastonbury Festival. As they neared Glastonbury, they saw the famous Glastonbury Tor on the horizon. Symon suggested they climb it to see the building at the top but Sid used one of his five pre-agreed vetoes on the grounds of being on holiday, not SAS boot-camp. Jimmy drove into the town and parked in the Abbey car park. He felt a little unnerved leaving the car alone for the first time since he'd got it working but knew it was something he would have to face at some time and perhaps doing so in sleepy Somerset was not a bad idea. They turned right out of the car park and headed up the high street. Sid sniffed loudly. Like a bloodhound following the scent of a killer, he took the lead. He nearly jogged for the next ten yards until he turned right into a small shop whose window was crammed with gems, pebbles, candles, dream catchers and other assorted paraphernalia. As they assembled inside, Sid sighed. "Joss sticks and patchouli oil! The companions of good dope all the world over!" Sean chuckled. "Crystals and crap! The companions of idiots all the world over!" Sid went straight for the bong section and picked up a particularly crappy plastic specimen but it had a picture of a marijuana leaf on the side so he was sold. Sean bought a small pair of crystal earrings. "A memento for Jo." He justified to nobody interested. Symon and Jimmy resisted the urge to buy anything though a book on lay lines nearly had Jimmy reaching into his pocket but instead he chose to keep his cash for beer supplies. They spent another hour in Glastonbury mainly placating Sid and Sean who for some strange reason had suddenly become interested in all things Wicca. Eventually Jimmy and Symon managed to persuade them to get back in the car and back on plan. Symon suggested just heading south and seeing where it lead them but Jimmy decided to go back the way they had come and get back on the A37 which would lead them to the A303 and the route to Exeter. Unfortunately, they went wrong at a roundabout near Shepton Mallet and found themselves on the A371. They were all starting to feel a bit peckish so stopped at The Natterjack Inn for a pint, some nosh and directions. The landlord welcomed them and provided menus and three pints of local cider for Sean, Symon and Sid and a pint of diet coke for Jimmy. Sid chose a vegetarian platter while Jimmy, Sean and Symon decided on fish and chips. The food came and they wolfed it down in no time. Jimmy was anxious to get back on the road so asked for directions while they each paid their share of the bill. Adrian, the landlord, told Jimmy to keep going in the direction he was, to turn right at Castle Cary train station and to follow that road till they reached a big set of traffic lights at Lydford. Turning left there would put them back on the A37 towards the south west. Within five minutes of setting off,

Bristle

Sid was moaning that he needed them to stop so he could pee. Jimmy was beginning to realise what hell he had been as a kid on family outings and laughed when he shouted back to Sid to "Grow up and hold on like a big boy!" Eventually, both Sean and Symon joined Sid in asking for a brief pee stop and Jimmy had no choice but to concede. He pulled over in a lay-by and stayed in the car while the others hopped over a gate and peed behind a hedge. Back on the road again, he pulled up to the Lydford traffic lights and turned left. The road from there was arrow straight apart from one or two undulations and minor squiggles due to it being an old roman road called the Fosse Way, or so Symon told him. How Symon knew was a question Jimmy could not be bothered to ask. Soon enough they reached a large roundabout and their first signs for the A303 and Exeter. The A303 was dual carriageway for the next few miles which, thankfully for Jimmy, meant that the 'kids' fell asleep after their large lunch and the local cider. By the time they woke up, Jimmy had got as far as where the A303 ended and the A30 began. He felt it unnecessary to let them know that he had 'opened her up' a little on the dual carriageway section and gently eased the speed up to 90 before his rapidly increasing heart rate reminded him to err on the side of caution and slow down to speeds he felt sure were within the car's abilities. The A30 bypassed Honiton and continued towards Exeter. They passed Exeter Airport and turned left onto the only stretch of motorway (M5) that Jimmy was willing to risk the car on. A few miles of Jimmy driving with his fingers crossed at a little over 80 brought them to the end of the M5 where it became the A38 and reduced back to single-lane carriageways. The road wound on for miles and miles as the scenery began to change to more moorland scenes interspersed with the odd village. Jimmy was beginning to relax about the car feeling that it had basically proved itself to be pretty reliable so far. At that precise moment, that the thought popped into his head, the engine coughed and the accelerator began to act like a slipper in a bucket of syrup. Jimmy flicked it into neutral and pulled off at the first chance which just happened to bring them to a pub on the left called The Dartbridge Inn with a massive car park. He pulled in and coasted to a halt in the far corner. He flicked the lever to open the bonnet and hopped out. Symon, Sean and Sid, who had provided nothing but financial help on the car decided to get out and provide technical assistance as Jimmy opened the bonnet and peered inside. "Are we out of petrol?" was Sid's useless question. "My Dad swears by WD40!" was Sean's addition. Symon thankfully didn't have a clue so instead asked "What do we do now?" Jimmy gritted his teeth and answered quietly, "Just

Bristle

get back in the car and sit on your respective asses while I try and find out what the problem is!" With the odd whispered "Ohh get him!" the lads did as they were told and got back in the car. Symon, though, realising he had been a little dickish by saying what he did, got into the driver's seat and shouted to Jimmy, "Just tell me when you want to try to start it again." Jimmy shouted back, "In a sec." and continued to look over the engine compartment. His gut feeling was that the carburettor had stuck or something similar. The fluids were all OK. He had been checking the fuel gauge regularly for the whole trip and was sure they were fine on that count. Deciding that there was no quick fix he went round to the side of the car and leaned in to speak to them all. "Look. It's not a quick fix. I think it's the new carb so I have to dismantle a few things and check it out. Why don't you go into the pub and have a pint or two while I look it over." Sid shouted "Result!" and got out. Sean rushed to catch him up while Jimmy opened the boot and got out his tools. Symon leant against the front wing and asked, "Do you need a hand Jimmer? I know I don't know squat about cars but I could be your wrench monkey if it helps?" Jimmy smiled. "Thanks Slymes but it's a one man job. Go have a pint. I'll join you in a bit for one and a catch up on the sitch." Symon shrugged and went to join the others.

Symon ordered a beer and turned to find Sean and Sid both sat texting their respective girlfriends. He looked around and found a fruit machine so decided to throw a few quid at it. Half an hour later with pockets full of pound coins from repeat jackpots, Symon felt a tap on his shoulder from Jimmy with a pint for him. They sat next to Sean and Sid who sent off a couple of quick texts and put their phones away. Jimmy took a large gulp of his beer before giving the lads the news. "Firstly, the carb is fine. No burning or excess fuel so that's good news. Bad news is that one of the fuel pipes has burst. I've clamped it, well bent it over and taped it, so we're not losing petrol but I need to find a local garage and get some more tubing. I've tried every one within walking distance and none of them have any spare but one has ordered it and promised they will receive it first thing ... tomorrow. So we have to find somewhere to kip tonight." Symon spoke. "That's good news then really. How about staying here? They've got rooms." Sid looked worried. "'Ang on a sec! Firstly, we're in yokel land here. I can just hear the banjos tuning. Secondly, we're in the land of the tourist now mate. They'll fleece ya for fun! Not sure my budget can cope with a hotel night. I've only really brought enough for drink." Sean piped up then. "I've checked, they have a brochure on the desk as you walk in, £70 per room per night. If they let us share it will still cost £140." Symon, Sid and

Bristle

Jimmy all scowled. "Looks like we'll have to find a field and set up camp then!" All four lads nodded and got up to walk out. As they crossed the car park, Jimmy spoke. "I didn't want to say anything in the pub in case the landlord overheard but if you look through the trees near where we parked, there's a field there. Might be spot on." They all grabbed their tents and rucksacks from the car and headed into the trees. After walking through some really tall nettles, Sid getting his elbows stung, they found themselves in the corner of a large field that looked perfect for a surreptitious camp site.

Camping

Sean and Jimmy got their tents up in no time and then helped Symon and Sid erect theirs. Sid and Sean offered to go find some wood for a fire while Symon and Jimmy unrolled sleeping bags and put out chairs. Quickly, Symon and Jimmy got bored waiting for the others so figured they'd try and find a river and catch their supper. Considering neither had ever been fishing apart from on holiday with crab lines and they had no fishing tackle, their plan had little chance of success. They had walked across two fields without even finding a river before deciding it was a stupid idea and turned back. Had they given this idea just a little more thought they might have realised that the pub in whose car park they had left the car being called 'The Dartbridge Inn' was a clue to how close they really were to a river, the river that was just on the other side of the road in the opposite direction to the field. On their way back they decided to pick up small sticks and potential kindling for the fire just in case Sean and Sid had neglected to do so. They needn't have worried as Sean being an accomplished hunter had started the fire while waiting for them. The four lads sat round the fire in their folding chairs with a tin of cheap lager each. Sean looked at his watch. "It's only four o'clock lads. What we gonna do?" The others shrugged. "What are we gonna do for food?" asked Symon. All four sat there thinking and sipping. Sean's face lit up like Blackpool illuminations. "How about we go for a dip in the river and maybe catch a trout or two?" Symon and Jimmy shook their heads. "We've been miles and couldn't find a river." said Jimmy. Sean looked incredulous. "Twats! It's just the other side of the road. Sid and me saw it when we got the firewood." Symon spoke, "You brought a fishing rod then Sean?" Sean shook his head. "Nah. Tickle 'em, my boy! Tickle 'em. So, we up for it then? Swim and a tickle?" Finding no immediate reason not to the other lads looked to Sean and shrugged their agreement. They disappeared into their tents and came out in swimming shorts, T shirt and sockless trainers. They followed Sean through the trees and across the road. Crawling over a few rocks got them to the river which was freezing or diabolically refreshing depending on your outlook. Thankfully it wasn't deep enough for a proper swim though the mud in places did a good job of sucking on their feet. Sean crept around looking for trout like a stork on the margins of Lake Victoria. Sadly, after about half an hour, he had caught nothing while the others had tired of their rapidly bluing feet and got back onto the rocks for a bit of sunbathing. "Shit! There's nothing in here. Possibly too shallow for them." Sean said making no attempt to hide his frustration. They all walked back to their camp site, shoes squelching as they went. They got out of their shorts, hung them up to dry and got into some form of suitable evening attire which in this case meant best jeans and a plain shirt. They sat and contemplated what to do. "So we need food and beer. We can't afford to have a meal at a pub or restaurant nor even drink there all night." Symon said resignedly. "How about we go see the landlord and explain our predicament and ask if he could sell us some cheap bits for us to cook ourselves and we stick to our cheap tinnies for tonight? We can buy some more at the next supermarket we pass." Jimmy suggested. "What if he realises we've parked the car in his car park overnight and gets all uppity?" asked Sid. "We'll have to take that risk." Jimmy replied. Nobody else could think of a better idea so they slowly got up and made their way to the pub. Thankfully the landlord was behind the bar so they didn't need to ask for him. Jimmy did the talking. "I wonder if you could help, sir. We're on a limited budget week away and much as we would love to dine at your wonderful pub, we don't have quite that kind of resources. I wondered if you might have some food that you don't want any more, perhaps you've changed to a new dish or something, that you would be willing to sell us for us to cook on our campfire?" The landlord looked Jimmy and the other lads over. "Nope." Jimmy looked crestfallen. He turned with the others to walk out. "But ... my dishwasher has called

Bristle

in sick and I've got a pile of logs out the back that need splitting. Two of you do the dishes, the others do the logs and I'll sort out some stuff for you to cook." The lads looked at each other and shrugged. Sid whinged under his breath, "Some holiday." but followed the landlord with the others. Pointing to Jimmy and Symon the landlord said "You two get an apron," he pointed to a pile of green aprons, "marigolds and get scrubbing." The pile of washing up was clearly not just from the lunchtime trade and perhaps was more than last night's too. Sean and Sid chuckled. "And you two follow me." the landlord said pointing to Sean and Sid. As they got outside the landlord pointed to the biggest pile of logs either of them had ever seen. "Come in when you've done them all." The landlord disappeared back into the pub. There were two small hatchets stuck in a large log on the floor next to the pile. Sean, having split logs all his life on the farm, grabbed the hatchets and threw one aside and said to Sid, "I'll split, you stack." Sid wasn't exactly sure what this meant but as Sean grabbed a log and deftly split it in two then each half in two again he nodded. Sid grabbed the four quarters and began the split stack up against a nearby wall. Inside, Jimmy had tied the apron around his waist which prompted a "Suits you, sir!" comment from Symon. Jimmy cleared the sink and filled it with hot water and fairy liquid. He grabbed a nearby brush and one by one began to clean the plates before placing them into a sink full of clean water. Symon rinsed them in the clean water and stacked them on the table behind him. And so it went for the next half an hour. It seemed to them both that the pile was barely reducing. The landlord had walked by a couple of times and said nothing to them. This time, he was carrying four open bottles of lager. He held one near Jimmy's face and motioned for him to open his mouth. Jimmy did so and the landlord poured a fair amount down his throat. He did the same for Symon before continuing outside where he passed a bottle each to Sean and Sid. He then walked back inside the pub without saying a word. And so the evening continued until finally the pile of dishes had disappeared, having been replenished a couple of times during the hours they worked. At that moment, Sid and Sean appeared wiping a good sweat of their brow. Jimmy and Symon removed their gloves and aprons and breathed a sigh of relief. All four lads leaned against the table and shook their heads. "Great night Jimmer!" said Sid. At that moment the landlord appeared from the kitchen with two boxes in his arms. "Follow me boys." He said as he walked through into the bar. The lads stood the customer side of the bar and took a stool each. The landlord poured four pints of beer and handed one to each. "Lads. I know you think you've been stiffed but you haven't, I promise. You got me out of a hole tonight so in appreciation of your efforts, here's a box of lamb chops and chicken breasts and a small steak each," he said patting the left box, "and here's a box of sausages, bacon and eggs for brekkie tomorrow." he said patting the right box. He reached under the bar and pulled out eight bottles of lager and placed them on top of the boxes. "Fair deal?" All the lads grinned and nodded enthusiastically. "Oh wow that's very good of you sir. Thank you so much." Jimmy exuded. "Absolutely, thanks a bunch." added Symon. Sean and Sid were busy swallowing their pints but mumbled their thanks equally loudly. "And we'll not worry about charging you overnight parking. Eh lads?" the landlord said with a wink. Jimmy turned a little red and smiled. They downed their pints and grabbed the boxes and bottles. Thanking him again, the four lads walked out of the pub, across the car park and through the trees which now it had gone dark were a different encounter altogether than earlier in the day. Back at the campsite Sean stoked the fire and got it hot. Jimmy handed him a frying pan with a small bottle of cooking oil and placed four plastic plates with forks on the floor beside the fire. "I'll be mother then, eh?" Sean said as he reached for the box with the steaks in it. He took a look inside and liked what he saw. He put the pan on a kind of griddle that he had made with some stones he'd got at the river and poured some oil in it.

He then pulled a knife from his pocket and flicked it open. He grabbed four bags from the box and slit each bag open. "Any condiments Jimmer?" Jimmy smiled and pulled packets of salt and pepper from his jacket pocket. Sean put a packet of salt and pepper on each side of each steak and threw them onto the smoking pan. After a few minutes he turned them over briefly then declared them done and forked one on to each plate. He then seasoned the chicken breasts and threw them in the pan before grabbing his steak in his fingers and tearing at it like a ravenous wolf. The other lads did likewise and moaned in ecstasy at their first taste of outdoor cuisine. Sean turned the chicken from time to time and when he thought they were done, used his fork to cut into one to check they were fully cooked through. They were, so he tossed one onto each plate. He seasoned the lamb chops and threw them into the pan. The lads chomped on the chicken like they had the steaks before and moaned again in an equally orgasmic manner. "Fuck me mate. You are the best cook ever!" Sid enthused. He had given up on his diet for the sake of peace and quiet, knowing it would be near impossible on a trip where everyone was roughing it. He would get back on it after the trip. Sean touched his fork to his forehead in salute to the compliment. The chicken was finished just as they lamb chops sizzled to readiness. Again they were flipped onto the awaiting

Bristle

plates and all four tucked in. Jimmy handed round opened bottles of lager and the four lads sat back in their chairs and looked out across the field. "Bugger me this is quality." Symon sighed. Jimmy looked across and smiled. Sean took a swig of his beer and agreed. "Quality idea this Jimmer." "Spot on." Agreed Symon and Sid, toasting Jimmy with their bottles. Jimmy smiled and bowed a little. They sat there for another hour just enjoying the moment and drinking the landlord's beers until unanimously they decided to hit the hay. One by one they disappeared into their own tents and quickly fell asleep.

The Journey Continues

The next morning Jimmy, Sid and Symon awoke to the smell of eggs, bacon and sausages. Sean had been up at the crack of dawn, unable to switch off his body clock, and had got the fire going again and started breakfast. Jimmy phoned the garage and hearing good news asked Sean to save him some breakfast while he went and got the tubing from the garage. Half an hour later, Jimmy returned and quickly polished off the remainder of the sausages, bacon and eggs. Symon offered to pack up his tent while he fixed the car. As Sean, Sid and Symon hoisted all the gear onto their backs and made their way through the small copse, they heard the welcome sound of the engine fire into life. Their huge cheer announced their arrival to Jimmy who got out of the car and held his hands aloft like a cup winning captain. They threw their stuff into the boot and hopped in. Jimmy gingerly drove them out of the car park and back onto the A38 towards Plymouth. The journey through Plymouth was uneventful. Even the brief trip through the Saltash tunnel which got Jimmy's heart racing a little, fearing a breakdown in the tunnel, proved plain sailing. After miles of requests to stop at the next supermarket, Jimmy pulled off at the Carkeel roundabout and quickly found a large Lidl. Jimmy stayed in the car but handed £20 to Symon who with Sid and Sean went in to the supermarket and twenty minutes later came out pushing a trolley filled with Praga Czech lager and Golden Goose ale. They opened the boot and filled it to the gunnels. Jimmy swore the car was a little sluggish after the supermarket trip with the extra weight on board but the lads would have none of it. Sean had used about £20 of the kitty to buy some food so that when they camped tonight they wouldn't have to worry. They continued on the A38 past Liskeard until it caught up with the A30 which took them south until they turned onto the A39 to Newquay. Jimmy was concentrating on his driving having never driven this far or long before. This meant he missed most of the lagers being passed from back to front and consumed by the three passengers. By the time they began to descend into central Newquay, the conversation had likewise headed to a new low.

Nookie in Newquay

"So where to first boys?" asked Jimmy with excitement as his first journey in the car neared its end and other than a burst pipe all his work had proved pretty good and the car relatively reliable. "Bitch!" slurred Sid. "You what?!" questioned Jimmy. "Beeeech!" repeated Sid. "Yeah take us to the BITCH my man!" Sean shouted. "Yeah, Fishall Beach!" agreed Symon. "You mean Fistral Beach?" clarified Jimmy. "Yeah!" the other three shouted in uniform agreement. Jimmy drove down Gannel Road, across the roundabout onto High Tower Road, round the gold course on Headland Road and parked up in the nearly empty car park facing the rolling surf. All four lads got out of the car and breathed in deeply. The day was moderately warm but the wind and spray coming off the sea was still bracing. "Swim!" shouted Sean. "Swim!" agreed Symon and Sid. "Are you three sure you're in a fit state?" asked Jimmy. "Oh fuck off Mum!" shouted Sid and went to the boot to get his trunks. Shrugging his shoulders Jimmy waited for them to get their still slightly damp trunks out of the car boot then got his own. They all got back in the car and changed. Jimmy locked the car and tied his shorts through the hole on the key before jogging to join up with the other three who were slightly zig-zagging across the beach. Thankfully the sea was pretty mild and there was no undertow to speak of so their swim

Bristle

was perfect to sober up Sean, Symon and Sid. Jimmy tried a bit of body-surfing and caught a couple of nice waves but most of all just relaxed after the pressure and tension of the long drive. After an hour messing about in the waves and another hour lying on the sand, the question arose as to a plan for the rest of the day. It was lunchtime so they were all feeling ravenous and thirsty. Jimmy suggested the Beach bar so they all grabbed a T shirt and trainers and walked across.

The summer holiday period hadn't fully kicked in so the bar was pretty quiet. There were a few clutches of people milling around but unlike the summer, they all seemed to be old enough to drink. Jimmy and the lads ordered a pint each and found a pair of comfortable sofas to lounge on. Having not drunk at all that day, Jimmy took a few beers to fully get into the holiday mood. The others though, soon topped up their pre-swim levels and began dancing in their seats to the background music. The conversation between Sean, Symon and Sid bored Jimmy so he kept out of it instead doing some people watching. He had marvelled at his boss Paul's easy manner around women and had often spoken to him about it. Paul had told him that the secret to being at ease around people was to have no agenda. This made no sense to Jimmy initially. Paul explained that if you started chatting to a girl and really what was going on in your head was 'How do I get this girl into bed?' then that would sour your time with her and steer the conversation down a route it didn't necessarily want to go rather than allowing the time to flow and the natural process to find its own way. So Jimmy had decided that on this trip he was not going to try and find a girl to shag. He had a girlfriend at home anyway so it was not the urgently critical feat that it was usually. Instead he would be casual and friendly. He would chat to girls like they were female mates and find out as much as he could about them. And so when one of the girls from the nearby gaggle looked his way, he just smiled and nodded a welcome then continued looking around. Symon was the only member of their group who currently didn't have a girlfriend but his looks, confidence and natural nonchalance invariably made him the centre of attention. Jimmy went up to the bar to buy the next round. He smiled at the barmaid and asked for four beers. She poured them quickly and placed them on a tray for him. He smiled again and said "Thanks." As he walked back to the lads with the beers, the girl from the nearby group walked past him. "Hi." he said as he smiled and continued his way. A couple of minutes later the girl returned and walked past the lads again. Jimmy motioned hello again with a slight nod of his head. She paused and asked "How did you find the waves this morning?" Jimmy assumed she thought them to be surfers. "Fun! But we're not surfers. We're just down here for a bit of a break. Beautiful beach though. I did a bit of body surfing but I am sure all you real surfers think that's just for kids." She laughed. "No, not at all. We're all closet boogers when it's blown out. Well actually, yeah ok, it is a bit for kids. You ever wanted to learn for real?" Jimmy shook his head. "I can't say I've ever really thought about it. I'd love to have a go but not sure my budget will stretch to all the gear or paying for lessons." At this point the girl's friends had got up and stood with her listening in. "Well we never pay for lessons. We help each other out. I've been teaching my little sister here," she put her arm around a girl who was a slightly shorter version of herself, "and she's picking it up pretty good. She's using an old wet suit of mine and one of my old boards." Jimmy smiled. "You reckon you have an old wet suit that I could fit in?!" Everyone laughed at that. Jimmy looked mock-shocked at the lads. "So when are you going out again?" Jimmy asked her. "Well it's all ankle-busters at the moment so not good for much but should be choka tomorrow. May be a bit too much for Barneys but worth a go." Jimmy looked a little confused but reckoned he got the gist of what she said. "Cool. What sort of time and where?" She smiled. "Outside here at 7?" Jimmy looked shocked. "In the AM?!" They all laughed. "Best waves are early."

Jimmy sighed. "7am it is then! So what do you do for the rest of the day? Where's the best place to go in the evening?" She chose this moment to introduce herself. "I'm Steph. This is my little sister Ginny." Then pointing at each as she went she introduced the other in the group who one by one raised their hand like answering role call in school. "This is Kate, Beth and Liz. That's Ben and Steve and finally Paige and Skye." Jimmy made the introductions for the lads. "I'm James, Jimmy or Jimmer, this is Symon, Sid and Sean." The lads all waved hello and shuffled up to make space for the others to sit with them. Ben and Steve grabbed another sofa and manoeuvred it to form a U shape around the table. As Jimmy and Steph started talking about what the locals did for fun when not surfing, the others all began finding out about each other. Ben and Steve were massive football fans so when they heard about Symon being an apprentice at Bristol Rovers, they monopolised his time entirely. At the first pause, Symon asked Ginny, who was squeezed between the two boys, what sport she liked. Ginny turned beetroot red and looked down at her hands. She whispered "Football. And I know all about you!" It was Symon's turn to blush and look confused. "How do you know all about me?" Ginny smiled. "You're Symon Shaw. You're from Wales and joined Rovers as an apprentice two years ago having been signed three years before that. You played for Southsea near Wrexham first. Your favourite food is chicken and chips, favourite band is Portishead and favourite colour is red after the team you've supported all your life, Liverpool. You play central midfield now but prefer to be more attacking." Symon sat there aghast, as did Ben and Steve. "How the hell?" mumbled Ben. "I'm a huge Rovers fan. Watched them all the time when we lived in Bristol. Dad used to take me before he lost his job and we moved down here." Symon closed his jaw. "Well I'm honoured to meet a true fan, Ginny!" Ginny smiled. "Just for the record, I'm not a stalker and for all Steph's talk of me being her *little* sister, I'm only 10 months younger than her and she's twenty two!" Symon laughed. "Fair comment then, Virginia." Ginny chuckled.

Sean and Sid were the filling in the sandwich between Kate, Beth and Liz. All three girls were incredibly chatty and in no time Sean and Sid were feeling the strain of turning from left to right all the time to answer their questions. Paige and Skye were sat cross-legged on the floor next to Steph, chatting to Jimmy. Paige mentioned a couple of clubs that they sometimes go to but that nothing much happened on Mondays. The night life picked up nearer the weekend. Skye said that often they'd just grab a few beers, set a big fire on the beach and have a casual beach party most nights. Jimmy said that sounded like a great idea. "How do we get that organised?" Steph turned to face everyone, "Beach Party tonight?" Everyone cheered enthusiastically. Ben spoke "I'll get some beers. Dad owns a pub in town so he's got some 'nearly out of daters' he'll let us have." Steve spoke next, "Paige and me'll get some goodies, eh Paige?" Paige smiled and nodded. "Mum owns the bakery so whatever's left from the day we can have." Sid looked at Paige, "Are you and Steve brother and sister then?" Paige smiled. "Step-brother." Skye and Liz, in unison, said "We'll get some veggies." Paige looked at Sid. "They're sisters. Their folks own a corner shop." Kate and Beth, who had been pretty quiet up till this point, spoke up. "We'll cook!" Ben said to Symon and Sid, "They go to the catering college in St Austell." pronouncing it 'snozzle'. Steph smiled at everyone's eagerness to be welcoming. "Sorted then."

Most of the group disappeared to run their errands leaving the lads, Steph and Ginny to go find a nice site. On their way across the beach, along the edge of the car park, Jimmy asked Steph, "How can we help? Shall we bring our tents and set them up so we can shelter if it gets cold? And we've got some food and drink and cooking stuff." Steph replied enthusiastically, "That'd be great." Jimmy added, "We can get changed out of

Bristle

our ... 'boardies' is it?" Steph nodded. "Great! You and Ginny find a spot and we'll change, grab some stuff and come find you." Steph and Ginny wandered off while Jimmy, Sean, Sid and Symon went back to the car to change and grab their camping gear. They got back on the beach and walked in the direction Steph and Ginny had gone. They found them within about 100 yards of the car park in a small alcove with dunes around it. The dunes sheltered them from the wind and provided a nice secluded spot with a great view of the sea. Symon and Jimmy set up the tents with the assistance of Steph while Sean, Sid and Ginny got some wood together and started the fire. Sean laid out the cooking gear while Sid arranged the bottles into lager and beer piles. As if knowing exactly where the campfire would be, the others arrived walking through the dunes instead of along the beach. It was obvious that beach parties like this were a regular affair as almost immediately a couple of tables were set up with various salad and breads on them. A small radio was turned on and tuned to a local station playing good dance music. More beers were added to the various piles and a couple of bottles of wine, some coke, lemonade and rum were placed on the tables along with a tube of paper cups and a stack of paper plates. Ben got out a couple of big black bags and hooked them onto the edge of the tables. "Don't wanna be a dick but we are allowed to party here because we make sure the place is tidy afterwards. Left bag for rubbish we can't burn, right bag for bottles and cans." Realising this comment was meant for them, Jimmy, Sean, Symon and Sid all nodded in unison. "No worries, will do." said Sean, passing Ben and Steve a bottle of Lidl lager. Jimmy manoeuvred Steph to one side at this point and not sure exactly how to say it, mumbled, "Umm. Look. They're good lads but they ... well they can get a bit ... drunk, quick." Wishing to not give the wrong impression, he quickly added, "Not violent. Just silly and well they may not end up being quite the tidy hosts you might hope for." Steph smiled. "Don't worry Jimmy. As long as you help me clear up in the morning, we'll be good." Jimmy breathed a sigh of relief. Steph punched him playfully on the arm. "Relax dude. Grab a beer." They walked back closer to the now raging fire. Everyone sat in a semi circle around the fire looking either at the dancing flames or out to sea. In no time little groups formed with each of the lads at the centre.

Steve and Paige asked Sid what he did in Bristol and what plans he had for the future. He was honest and told them he basically had no idea. He was killing time at college really and the recent mishap had made him think about the future and what direction he wanted his life to take. He explained about the BAe legacy and how all his family had worked there for generations. Steve understood exactly what Sid meant. He talked about how his family had been pushing him to find a career and plan for it since he was 14 and started working towards qualifications. He said, "It's so unfair! I still haven't got a clue what I want to do but they expected me to know when I was barely able to understand what life was about. Don't get me wrong, I know you have to work to live but should you really have to live for work? I've seen what happens when you change your life to suit an ideal of what you want when you really don't have a clue. Dad could have been a professional rugby player if he hadn't given it up to give him the time to take more exams and get more qualifications so he could go to university and get a degree and then live a boring life always ruing that he wasted the time he had when he was young enough to enjoy it. He doesn't say that because he thinks its bad advice for me but I know he feels it. He could have had fun from 14 to 25 and THEN settled down. That's the way it should be. That's the way I'm going to do it. I'm saving up for a year or two abroad. Obviously I'll have to do crap jobs to feed myself but doing a crap job at night and surfing the best waves in the world during the day seems a fair price to me. Paige just listened to the two lads moans. Eventually Sid turned to her and asked what she wanted from life. She just smiled. "I know it sounds terribly old fashioned but I don't ever want a career or anything like that. I want a nice home life, kids round me ankles and cooking tea for hubby. Sad isn't it?" Sid and Steve both shook their heads in disagreement. "If that's what you want then its right." said Sid. Ben, Beth and Sean sat a little away from the rest. Beth asked Sean how the four of them met. He related their first day at College and how it had grown from there. He talked about how they came to buy the car and how they rebuilt it. Then Sean talked about the farm and how even though he had never wanted to really be a farmer, he loved the outdoor life and now that the farm was going to be sold, even that choice had been taken away from him. Beth nodded. "My family were fishermen but foreign competition and dwindling stocks put them out of business. He had to give up what he loved and all he knew and find a job doing anything just so we could make ends meet. He started stacking shelves at the supermarket and now he is assistant manager. He might not have the job he loved but he has pride in what he does." Ben had been listening intently though he knew the story from previous conversation with Beth. He realised they were both waiting for him to tell his story. "Oh my folks had me late in life. They both had high powered jobs in the city so as soon as I was born they upped sticks and retired to here.

Skye and Liz are from London too. Their story is different though. Very sad." Beth nodded.

Ginny and Symon had clearly taken an immediate liking to each other and sat nearly touching facing Skye and Liz. Symon talked a little about life as an apprentice footballer but began to feel a little uncomfortable as it always sounded like bragging to him so he ended his part of the conversation by suggesting, "But if you really want to know all about me, just ask Ginny!" she chuckled embarrassedly. "So tell me about you two? How did you come to Cornwall?" Ginny's smile immediately disappeared as Skye and Liz turned suddenly serious. "Oh I'm sorry. Have I said the wrong thing?" a concerned Symon asked. Liz spoke. "No, no. It's just ... well it's not exactly a nice story. Though it did get us here and we love every day so perhaps it's not the sad tale we've grown to believe." Symon nodded. "Well only if you feel you want to. Tonight's a party and I don't want to be the cause of ruining it." Liz smiled. "Well we all lived in London. The East End. Clapham. We had loads of friends and relatives around us and a lovely school ... and a lovely sister. Without going into too much detail, there was a shooting. The local corner shop got robbed and Iz just happened to be in the wrong place at the wrong time. A stray bullet caught her and by the time the ambulance arrived she was unconscious. She never came out of the coma." Symon looked mortified. "Oh I'm so sorry! I shouldn't have asked. What an awful thing to happen!" Skye smiled at his kind words. "Well, not long after that, Mum and Dad decided London was too dangerous so they sold up and moved us here, nearly as far away from London as we could get without going North! And we do love it here." Symon looked confused as a wrinkle slowly walked across his brow. "And your folks own a corner shop? Isn't that a bit ... well I don't know the word for it." Liz and Skye in unison replied, "Ironic?" Liz continued, "Yeah very. But I guess in a strange way they did it so that they could perhaps make sure it never happened to another family. They never said that the owner of the corner shop in London had done anything wrong, he certainly hadn't brought the shooting upon himself, but perhaps they feel they would have reacted quicker or differently or something. I don't really know. We've never talked about it." Symon nodded. "I guess it doesn't matter what it takes to overcome grief as long as you find it." Skye and Liz got up. "Time for us to make some salad and stuff." They shouted over to Kate and Beth. "Oi chefettes! Pull ya fingers out." Kate and Beth got up and began to prepare the food for cooking. Ginny nudged Symon and said, "Do you fancy going for a walk along the beach while they cook?" Symon smiled and got up. He reached out to help Ginny up and they walked off towards the far end of the beach.

Steph asked Kate before she went off to do the cooking with Beth if there was anything she could help with. Kate smiled and said, "No honey. We got it covered." Steph turned to Jimmy and smiled. "Feeling hungry?" Jimmy nodded. "I have to be honest, I'm a bit concerned about surfing tomorrow!" Steph laughed. "You'll be fine. I'll make sure you don't drown." and winked. "I could drown?!" Jimmy screamed in mock panic. "Now I'm REALLY afraid!" They laughed comfortably together. Steph watched Symon and Ginny walk off down the beach. "What's he like?" Jimmy followed her stare. "Symon? He's a nice lad. He's a bit mixed up at the moment. I think he's been skating along on natural talent so far and is finally beginning to realise that if he doesn't knuckle down and actually work at his game then he'll be just another would-be footballer who gets his kicks playing non-league. He's so good though! It would be such a waste if he didn't do his best. He really could be a Premier League footballer for one of the big sides if he just trained properly, gave up the occasional weed and cut back on the beer. But nobody can tell him that. It's a decision only he can make." Steph nodded. "Very true. Well if he does get with Ginny, she'll sort him out."

Jimmy laughed. "She's pretty formidable eh? But you still worry about her, don't you?" Steph agreed. "Course I do. She's my little sister. Always has been and always will be."
Ginny put her arm through Symon's as they walked. "So what are you going to do?" Symon looked across at her confused. "What do you mean?" Ginny smiled. "Well Rovers have kicked you out haven't they?" Symon laughed. "I should have realised. Of course you know!" Symon spent the next few minutes explaining why he'd been kicked out but also the other factors behind him feeling it was fully justified. He told her that he was beginning to struggle as other lads grew stronger and fitter. She gently pinched his tummy fat. "And the beer isn't helping is it?" Symon looked open mouthed at her. "Cheeky! But no, it's not helping." Ginny turned serious. "So tell me about football. What does it mean to you?" Symon thought for a minute. "I've always loved it. I would need to consult a psychiatrist to really tell you why. All I can say is that when I am out on the pitch with the ball at my feet or making a tackle or shooting, I'm in heaven on earth. My mind has nowhere else to be and is only thinking about the game. Any troubles I'm having at home or college or family ... they disappear." Ginny nodded. "So let me get this straight. The only thing in life that makes you happy is something you are risking because NOW you have to work at it?" Symon went quiet.

"You have the chance to do what others only dream of and that chance has been given to you in the form of a natural talent. Piss that away and you'll get no sympathy when you come back from working at Sainsbury's and moan about your job. You'll DESERVE no sympathy when you complain you are always under the cloud of 'family issues' and money worries. You've got a chance that perhaps one in a million get, the chance to do what you love for as long as your body can do it. And then you could probably stay doing something similar until you retire. You could have such a good life." Symon remained quiet. "Let me ask you a question. When you dribble through a bunch of players and decide to shoot, what goes through your mind? In that fraction of a second before you swing your foot and kick the ball, what do you imagine?" Symon stopped and turned to face Ginny. "I imagine my foot contacting the ball and catching it perfectly. I imagine the path of the ball and picture it arcing through the air, over the diving keeper and making the net bulge." Ginny smiled. "Exactly!" Symon grunted in confusion again. "You picture what you need to happen. You imagine every aspect of what is needed to attain the desired result. You set out your target and how to attain it. It might happen in a fraction of a second when you shoot but it's still the same process. So treat playing football as the goal. Now plan how to achieve it. Plan how you are going to contact the ball or career-wise, what you need to do to get regular first team football. Plan the trajectory of the ball or in this case what steps you need to take to keep your place in the side and be a benefit to your current club and a target for bigger clubs. Imagine the net bulging as the ball passes over the keeper or for your career, every Friday being the first name on the team sheet and every Saturday being in the middle of that pitch playing a part in the success of the team and club." They reached the end of the beach and automatically turned back. They both fell silent. They had nearly reached the bonfire when Symon stopped Ginny and put his hands on both her shoulders, turning her to face him. "Why haven't I thought of it that way? Why have I been fucking about for so long?" Ginny smiled. "You might be a genius on the pitch but sometimes you need one in your corner too." She reached up and gave him a peck on the cheek before turning towards the bonfire and walking off. Symon looked after her, deep in a myriad of new thoughts. A few minutes later he heard a shout. "Grub's up everyone. Grab a plate. There's salad, bread and some charred bits of meat on the tables." There was a loud grunt as Kate and Beth simultaneously elbowed Ben in the ribs. "Um I mean there's some succulent, perfectly cooked, *Gordon bloody blue* meat awaiting your highly tuned taste buds." This time he was expecting their

Bristle

elbows and danced out of the way but tripped on a box behind him and fell hard into the sand. Everyone burst out laughing including Ben. They formed an orderly queue by the tables and each took a small amount of salad, a roll or piece of French stick and a piece of meat. "Aren't we all polite tonight!" Steph announced. Turning to Jimmy she said, loud enough for all to hear, "Usually it's a complete bun fight! Food flying everywhere!" They moved off and sat a little distance from the bonfire. Steph took a bite of French stick and asked Jimmy, "So tell me about girls." Jimmy looked at her. "Well, they're weird creatures that are supposedly human ..." Steph laughed. "No! Cheeky! I mean tell me about girls in your life." Jimmy faked surprised realisation. "Ohhhh! Well let me see." He decided upon full honesty for his answer. "There are four girls in my life. First there's my Mum who is a complete nutter that apparently enjoys dogging and younger men while Dad watches but that's another story all of its own. Secondly there's my sister who works on the perfume counter at Lewis's and has had the worst luck with men. Though for some reason she's been a lot happier lately. Then there's Jennifer." Jimmy paused to work out exactly how he could describe her. "She's a girl that I have seen nearly every day for two years and spoken to once. She's been the centre of my amorous dreams for all that time while also being my white whale and Everest. Then there's Jo. She's a nurse I met in a bar a couple of weeks ago who I've gone out with twice. We had an evening bowling, a good laugh and a fairly substantial snog. That's pretty much it." Steph smiled. It was obvious that Jimmy had answered fully and honestly. "So tell me about Jennifer first. Why so ... chicken about it? Why have you not taken the plunge and asked her out?" Jimmy chuckled. "Well she always seemed so unattainable. You girls think it's so easy for us blokes because of how often we hit on you. But you don't see that the nice guys, the normal, ordinary guys, don't find it easy. You don't see the hours of plucking up courage or in most cases, drinking courage Dutch or otherwise!" Steph laughed out loud. "Oh you poor baby! You're right! Your life is so much harder than us girls! We don't really risk being called a slut if we ask out a bloke. We don't risk the bloke immediately thinking 'I'm on here – shagville here we come' at all! We don't have to be subtle and sit there making occasional eye contact, trying to look sexy, coquettish, alluring, interesting and welcoming all at once do we? Sheesh!" It was Jimmy's turn to laugh. "You do all those things?" Steph smiled. "Well not all at once! We try to use the minimum tool needed for the job! OK, so what about Jo? How did you manage to pluck up the courage to go out with her?" Jimmy shrugged. "As previously stated, if lacking courage naturally, drink some, Dutch preferably but anything alcoholic will work." Jimmy went on to explain exactly how he met Jo and the calamitous events of that first evening. "So what are your intentions with Jo?" asked Steph. "Not sure really. I'm working on what I call the 'Paul approach'. Paul's my boss and he always seems so ... comfortable around women. Actually he's comfortable around everyone. He reckons that talking to people with a specific agenda in mind kills the conversation and ruins the chances of having a good conversation. He believes that just being natural and actually being interested in what the other person has to say is the best way to enjoy your time with whomever you are spending it. Radical, eh?" Steph nearly choked with laughter as she sipped from her beer bottle.

Paige was feeling just a little buzzed from her beers and wanted some entertainment. "Did you bring it, Ben?" she shouted across the dunes. He looked across at her and nodded. "Yay!" she shouted. "We want music!" Ben shook his head. "You know I can only play not sing. If you want the full song then you'll have to persuade Skye to sing." Everyone looked to Skye who turned a little red but smiled and nodded. "Oh OK." Ben got up and reached behind the tables and got out his guitar case. Inside was a beautiful 12 string with inlaid pearl blocks on the neck. He pulled a small stool out from his guitar case and put it on the sand a few yards back from the fire. He sat down and looped the strap over his shoulders. He strummed once across all the strings, made some minor adjustments, played a lightning fast excerpt from 'The Chain' by Fleetwood Mac to check the bass strings, then played a minute of Moonlight Sonata the incredibly complicated third movement intended for piano but awesome on a guitar and looked up. "What's your poison Skye?" Skye thought for a second before replying, "Let's start with Hotel California." Ben immediately began playing the iconic opening guitar solo that made Hotel California so famous. Skye stood up and moved over to stand next to Ben where she started gently swaying in time with the tune. Skye's voice was amazing. Only the members of the group who had heard her sing before knew that she was mimicking the voice of Don Henley with his slightly gravely but melodic voice. The four lads just sat there drooling at the quality of both the guitarist and singer in front of them. Without taking his eyes from the duo, Jimmy whispered unintentionally "Amazing!" to which Steph leaned over and whispered in his ear, "They are. She doesn't know what a talent she has and you've heard nothing yet. He was classically trained but can play anything after hearing it once. Genius really." The song neared its end and Ben improvised a riff that followed the original tune but was somewhere between heavy rock and orchestral classical. Skye looked down at Ben and nodded. He knew what she wanted to sing next. The song was instantly recognisable though how Ben managed to play a song so synonymous with the piano on a guitar was beyond belief for Jimmy. Skye started singing in a deep rich voice that had they not had the proof before their eyes the four lads would have sworn was Adele. She powered through the chorus of 'Someone Like You' with apparent ease while Sid sat there and nearly applauded. As the song ended, Paige spoke out. "Can we have something to dance to?" Skye scowled. "We'll put the radio back on and you can dance to that." Paige, realising she was the only one who wanted to dance, sat down and shut up. It wasn't that she didn't love listening to Skye and Ben it was just that she was in the mood to boogie. Skye and Ben continued for another half an hour with songs from the fifties up to modern day. Finally, Skye felt tired and took a bow and a round of applause before sitting back down with the rest of the group. Ben, still feeling in the mood to play, began to go through his repertoire of classical guitar pieces. The conversations started again but slightly hushed. An hour later and Ben recognised the yawns slowly increasing around the group. He said quietly, "Last one then I'm off home." and began to play

Romanza. The waves rolling up against the sand became a gentle rhythmic background with the occasional crackle from the fire adding musical accents. To say it was the perfect way to end the evening would be an understatement of magnificent proportions. The conversations again tailed off as everyone sat and listened. As the last few notes tailed into the night, Ben packed up his guitar and stretched his back. Everyone began to clear up and fill the black bags. The fire had a couple more hours in it so Steve asked Jimmy, "Are you lot camping here tonight or shall I put the fire out?" Jimmy looked to the lads who either shrugged or nodded. "Yeah we'll camp here." He looked to Steph as Symon looked to Ginny. Ginny smiled and looked to Steph who returned her smile. Everyone else, after a round of hugs and promises to see them tomorrow on the beach, wandered off into the dunes. Sean wished everyone a good night and ducked into his tent. Sid was stood looking out to the sea just staring, thinking and digesting their first evening. Symon and Ginny, holding hands, bent over and shuffled into his tent. Jimmy looked to Steph, "At least we're both going to be late for my lesson tomorrow!" Steph laughed as she kneeled and crawled into his tent. "Neither of us are going to be late. It's straight to sleep and my body clock will wake us up in plenty of time." Jimmy laughed and slapped her ass as he followed her on hands and knees into the tent. Steph took off her jumper, jeans and shoes and unzipped the sleeping bag. Jimmy did likewise and got into the now crowded sleeping bag with her. He zipped it up behind them and cuddled up to Steph's back as she turned away from him. They spooned until sleep overtook them.

The next morning Jimmy awoke to find Steph sat next to him putting her trainer shoes back on. "Smells like someone is cooking brekkers!" she said as she crawled outside throwing "Don't dawdle – surfing in 30!" over her shoulder. Outside Sean sat cross-legged in front of a smaller fire made from the embers of the previous nights'. He had a frying pan filled with sausages, bacon and eggs sizzling away on it. He looked up at Steph and with a wry smile asked, "Sleep well?" She smiled, realising his implication. "Dunno what he's like back in Bristol but in Newquay he's a perfect gentleman." She pinched a sausage from the frying pan and tossed it from hand to hand while blowing on it before biting a healthy chunk off it. "Anyone else up?" she asked. Sean motioned with his head to the beach in front of the fire where Sid sat hugging his knees. "I don't think he's slept." he whispered. Steph mouthed her surprise but said nothing. She walked over to Symon's tent and asked to the canvas door, "Surfing?" She heard a scuffle inside then the zip opened halfway and Ginny's head stuck out. "Give me a minute." Then another head popped out above it and Symon corrected, "Give US a minute." They both fell back inside giggling. Steph shook her head and walked back to the fire just as Jimmy crawled out and stood up stretching. He shuffled his feet and pretended to do some stretching as if preparing for a big football match. Seeing the pan full of cooked sausages, bacon and eggs now resting on the sand next to the fire, he enthused, "Ooooh! Sossies!" He rushed over, grabbed a sausage, wrapped it in two rashers of bacon, wrapped a fried egg around it and shoved it all into his mouth mumbling "Yum, yum!" as he devoured it. Jimmy spotted Sid sat alone on the beach. He looked at Sean and mouthed, "What's with Sid?" as he motioned his head toward the crouched figure. Sean shrugged. At that moment, Symon and Ginny bundled out of his tent. Jimmy saw the smile on his face and realised he'd not seen him look that happy in over a year. They came over to Sean, Steph and Jimmy. "How're the waves then teach?" Symon asked Steph. Jimmy tilted his head to where Sid was sitting. Symon looked across. "What's up with him?" he whispered. Everyone shrugged. Sean stood and came closer. "You lot go off surfing. I'll have a chat with him and we'll catch up with you in a bit." Steph asked, "Are you sure?" Sean nodded. "No worries." She gave his

Bristle

shoulder a gentle punch. "Thanks Sean." Symon slapped him avuncularly on the face. "Good lad!" Ginny passed Symon a sausage with hers sticking out of her mouth. The two happy couples thanked Sean again and set off along the beach. Everyone from the night before was on the beach in wetsuits waiting for them. "Waves look good for beginners." said Ben after the welcomes were complete. "Bugger!" laughed Jimmy. Steph giggled. "Have you two got spare boards for the boys?" she asked Ben and Steve. They nodded and motioned to the wall of the car park where two boards were leant. "Thanks. We've no spare wetsuits so you'll just have to keep yourselves warm. Ginny and me'll be back in a minute." Steph and Ginny rushed off to the changing rooms while Ben and Steve grabbed the spare boards and handed them to Symon and Jimmy. By the time Steph and Ginny returned, Ben and Steve had gone through a few safety tips and conduct rules with Jimmy and Symon. Like a well oiled machine they nodded to Steph and Ginny to say they'd prepped the newbies and handed them over to their instructors for the day. The whole group walked into the sea but Steph and Ginny held Jimmy and Symon back in the shallows. After an hour of coaching that would normally have been half an hour but Jimmy and Symon were having so much fun playing the fool, the girls led them out into the deeper surf. Jimmy struggled but by lunchtime had caught a wave and ridden it for about ten seconds which he found exhilarating but draining. Symon however, was a natural. The natural balance and ability of a good sportsman shone through and he took to it like a pro. By the end of the session, he was cutting through the waves and riding them until they melted into the sand. The rest of the group came over and they all walked in. As they neared the cafe, they saw Sean and Sid who had thoughtfully brought towels and dry clothes for Jimmy and Symon. The locals went in to the changing rooms to shower and change while Symon and Jimmy just dried off while chatting to Sean and Sid. "You OK mate?" Jimmy asked Sid. "Yeah mate! Course! Just been thinking through things. That was the purpose of this trip and it's exactly what I've been able to do." Symon patted him on the shoulder. "As long as you're ok?" Sid smiled. "Never been better." Jimmy and Symon went into the changing rooms to get into their dry clothes while Sean and Sid went in to the beach bar and ordered a round for everyone. Sid treated them.

That afternoon meandered quietly towards the evening with lunch and relay-snoozing being the occasional and only interludes. As the evening drew closer Sid's mind turned to more nocturnal activities and asked what the plan was. Ben looked up when nobody came forth with any bright suggestions. "How about a lock-in?" Everyone seemed up for it so it was decided. Steve asked "How about some fish and chips for tea before we start?" Symon, who was feeling particularly hungry shouted "Fish supper! Yeah!" Everyone laughed but nodded in agreement. They all stood and walked out of the bar toward the town centre with Symon, Sean, Sid and Jimmy following the others. Jimmy turned to Steph and asked, "Is my car safe in the car park?" Steph replied, "Your car? I thought it was a joint thing?" Jimmy corrected himself. "Well, yeah, it is." Steph smiled. "I'm sure it will be fine. It's not the busy season and it's the last place car thieves would look." They arrived at the chippy and one by one placed their orders. Before going on to the pub, they sat on a nearby wall and ate their fill from the warm, newspaper wrapped meals. "OK folks. Off to the boozer." said Ben as he lead them down the back streets. A few minutes later and they all piled into the pub. Ben went straight to the bar and had a brief chat with his Dad. In two minutes he came back and said, "Sorted. There's nobody in the back snug so it's ours for the night. It's an honesty bar cos he trusts me so if you're in agreement, we'll tally till we're done then split the bill." This was Jimmy's first lock-in so he looked quizzically to Steph for clarification. "He means we write down on a piece of paper what we drink and nobody takes the piss." Jimmy nodded in understanding. "Ahhh OK. I'll pass it on." He stepped over to Sean, Symon and Sid to explain the rules. They all nodded as they followed Ben through to the back. The rear snug was warm and comfortable with lots of chairs and sofas. Steve and a couple of the girls reorganised the furniture so enough seats were around enough tables to accommodate them all. Ben stood behind the bar and said "The first and last round is on me. That way I decide when we've had enough. Deal?" Symon looked over. "You sure Ben? We're all happy to pay our way." Ben shook his head. "It's no problem Sly. We're happy to have your company. So what'll it be?" One by one everyone shouted out their orders. Steve ferried the drinks out to the tables and everyone got comfortable. "So what did you guys think of surfing?" Steph asked Jimmy and Symon. "Oh great fun!" replied Symon enthusiastically. "I could really get into it!" Jimmy scowled. "That's only cos you're bloody brilliant at it! Typical sportsman – everything comes easy!" Jimmy laughed. "It was bloody difficult for me but I enjoyed it. Can't see it becoming anything more than a holiday activity though. Unless I move somewhere hot! Too cold in England!" he added. Steph and the others laughed. "Well you didn't have wetsuits on! That makes a big difference." Jimmy tutted. "Hah! I don't really want to do any activity where I have to wear something skin-tight that I have to piss in before I feel warm!" Steph looked at Ginny. "Before you ask, no I didn't teach him that!" Ginny chuckled. "Symon did take to it quickly though. Very good for football you know?" she said looking directly at Symon. "It builds up your ankle and calf-muscles as well as improving your balance on the ball." Symon laughed. "Is that why all the best footballers are surfers?" Ginny looked confused. "They are?" Symon nudged her. "Course not!"

The evening continued in a very civilised manner without too much drinking and nobody, possibly because of the large portion of fish and chips, felt even remotely drunk. At one point, nearing the end of the evening, about two hours after closing time when they had the entire pub to themselves but still stayed in the rear snug, a comfortable silence fell upon the group before Sean, from nowhere, began talking about the time when he had to dispatch a rabbit which led on to him talking about his father. "After I had to do that, kill the rabbit with my bare hands, I began to think about my Dad. I'm not sure why I had never thought about it before. Perhaps it was because I wasn't old enough to have an opinion. Perhaps it is because lately I've been thinking about the future and whether I would be a good father, a family man, a good husband. So I started to evaluate

his role. It left me wondering what exactly makes someone a good father. If it's someone who supports his family and puts food on the table then he's been a good father. If it is someone who is concerned about the future for his kids then he's been a good father. But, if it is someone who sees each child as an individual and adjusts what he says and does to suit then perhaps he has failed on that front. I think, from my perspective, he has been a good father but not a great one. You know the funny thing? I would never have questioned this at all if he hadn't told me to kill the rabbit that he had wounded. Perhaps it is when we see the chinks in the armour, the frailties in those we thought perfect, that we begin to judge. Perhaps it is the natural order of things that when the head of the household falters and the eldest son comes of age, one begins to slowly swap roles. Dunno." He spoke as if talking to himself but everyone had been sent into a silent reverie, no doubt contemplating their own families. "On that note, last orders folks." Jimmy stood up and walked to the bar. "Nothing more for me thanks Ben, I'm done. What's the damage?" Symon, Sean and Sid stood up and came over to the bar. As Ben totted it all up, Jimmy motioned to the others and they nodded. When Ben said "£80", each lad handed Jimmy a twenty and he placed £80 on the bar. "Our treat Ben. You've all made us very welcome and it's only right." Ben tried to

Bristle

argue but Jimmy and the lads put their wallets in their pockets and turned away. "Club tomorrow night?" asked Symon. Paige was the first to jump up excitedly and shout "Yeah! Boogey-night!" The others laughed but nodded agreement. Steph stood and came over to Jimmy. "No lesson tomorrow but I'll see you at the beach bar?" Jimmy nodded. He gave her a quick hug and thanked her for a great night. "Night all. See you tomorrow." He shouted over her head to the others. Ginny and Symon were leant against the wall kissing. As Jimmy, Sean and Sid passed, they grabbed Symon by the shirt collar and tugged him with them. He reluctantly released Ginny and followed them out of the pub with Ben unlocking the front door and giving directions back to the beach. The fresh bracing air hit them the moment they got outside. They strode purposefully back to the beach and their tents. Without a further word, each disappeared into their tents and immediately fell asleep.

"What time is it?" Sid said sleepily as he was awoken by Jimmy shaking him. "4am." Sid paused. "What the hell are you waking me up for at 4 frigging am?" Jimmy knelt next to him. "Sean's just got a phone call. It was from the police. It seems that sometime last night, his sister went out to the milking parlour to find her Dad because he hadn't come back to the house and she ... well she found his body.

He'd shot himself. His sister and Mum are obviously too upset to talk so we've got to get back there pronto." Sid blinked. "Fuck! How's he taken it?" Jimmy looked seriously at Sid. "Very well considering. He's clearly shocked but so far hasn't shown how upset he must feel." Sid unzipped his sleeping bag. "OK. Give me five minutes and I'll be ready to go." Jimmy crawled out of the tent as Symon crawled out of his, dressed and packed. He started dismantling his tent and packing up the camping gear. Sean was stood, fully clothed, staring out to sea. Symon and Jimmy packed Sean's clothes and tent up while Sid did his own. They grabbed all their gear checking around to make sure the place was all clean then set off towards the car. Sid walked to Sean and placed his hand on his shoulder. "Ready?" he whispered. Sean looked round at him and nodded. They threw their stuff into the boot and got in. Jimmy fired up the car, reversed out of the parking bay and set off through the empty streets of Newquay. Jimmy drove safely but quickly through the dark streets and empty lanes. He missed the turn onto the A38 on purpose knowing from his route planning for the trip down that the A30 was the quickest way to the M5. Soon they reached the M5 and headed north. Jimmy put his foot down and cruised at just over 90 for the majority of the journey.

Bristle

The Return

"I need petrol. Anyone know where the next services are?" Jimmy asked. Symon looked around having not paid much attention to the journey so far. He knew the motorways and services locations pretty well because they always stopped at them on away trips for Bristol Rovers youth team. "Sedgemoor. About 10 miles." Jimmy relaxed at the news that he wasn't going to run out of petrol on such an important trip. The 10 miles passed quickly and he turned off the motorway following the winding road to the petrol station. Symon got out and went in to the shop to pay for the petrol and buy some 'goodies' while Jimmy filled the tank. Sid hopped out of the car and jogged to Starbucks for a coffee run. Jimmy finished filling the car and opened the bonnet to check oil and water levels. This was the first time he had driven the car for a fair journey at speed so he wanted to check it had coped with it. He was closing the bonnet as Symon and Sid returned. Jimmy buckled his seatbelt and they set off, Symon passed out crisps and chocolate bars to everyone. Sid handed out the coffee. Symon bit into his Mars bar and sighed as the sugar boost hit him. "The roads are never going to be quieter Jim. How about you see what she can do?" Jimmy looked across at him and a devilish smirk crossed his lips. As he accelerated back on to the motorway he kept his foot down and steadily increased their speed. In no time the speedo edged past 100 and kept rising. The engine sounded smooth. They sped through 110 and 120 with ease. Symon sat a little more upright and leant across to watch the speedo climb. Sid and even Sean sat upright in their seats and craned their necks to watch. The handling was smooth and the car seemed to eat up the road without difficulty. Everyone held their breath as the speedo touched and then rose past 130 before slowing. Jimmy had his foot flat to the floor. His concentration was at its highest. He was looking ahead at a completely empty motorway. Slowly, inexorably the speedo neared 140 miles per hour. With a fraction of an inch to go, Jimmy took his foot off the accelerator and shouted "Shit!" He pressed the brakes enough to slow down rapidly but not enough to skid. The speedo fell to 100 mph rapidly but it was too late. They sped past the police car on a small mound beside the carriageway just as it set off and immediately turned on its sirens and lights. Jimmy kept slowing down and pulled on to the hard shoulder indicating as he did so. "Fuck! That's my licence gone!" He started banging his head against the steering wheel in frustration. Behind them the police car pulled to a stop. A fully uniformed officer got out of the passenger side, pulled on his hat and hi-vis vest and walked up to the passenger side of the car. He bent over and looked inside before tapping on the passenger window. Symon pressed the button and prayed that the window would work. It did and rolled down perfectly. The police officer rested both hands on the window surround and looked inside. "Bit of a hurry eh lads?" Symon looked down at the officer's hands. "Can I have a quiet word officer?" he asked. The officer paused then nodded and backed away from the door. Symon got out leaving the other three lads wondering what he was going to say. Sid was sweating that the car would be searched as he had a bit of weed and his newly acquired bong stashed in his rucksack. Sean was anxious for obvious reasons. Jimmy was still shaking from the adrenalin of driving fast and the panic of potentially losing his licence. He leant across and looked out of the window. The officer and Symon had walked further on to the verge. The officer pulled out a mobile phone and dialled a number. He held the phone to his ear and spoke but Jimmy was too far away to hear what was said. The officer nodded to the person on the other end of the phone then ended the call and put the phone away. He paused for a few seconds then said a few words to Symon who turned and walked back to the car. As he got in, he buckled up his seat belt and without looking at Jimmy said, "Sorted. Off you go Jimmy." Jimmy began to mumble a question but Symon held up his hand. "Just drive." They set off and for the last half an hour of the journey, Symon would not be drawn on what had happened. They pulled off the motorway and drove through the streets of north Bristol for five minutes before arriving at Sean's family farm. Sean got out and walked slowly towards the house. His sister rushed out and jumped into his arms followed by his Mum who just hugged them both. Sid got out and grabbed Sean's rucksack and camping gear from the boot. He walked over to the farmhouse and put them down by the door. As he walked back past Sean he patted him on the shoulder and continued to the car. Jimmy turned the car around and they set off to Southmead.

The funeral

A week later, Jimmy, Symon and Sid sat in the car, dressed in their most sombre clothes, drove behind the hearse from the farm to the crematorium. On arrival, Jimmy quickly parked the car and the three of them walked briskly to the back of the hearse where Sean was waiting with a weak watery smile. "Thanks for this lads." he whispered in greeting. "Not a problem." Sid replied as he took the handle of the coffin. Sean and Sid stood at the front, Jimmy and Symon behind and two more pallbearers from the funeral company took the rear. The funeral director faced them and in a quiet but confident voice, with his hands guiding them, said "Ready? Now lift." All six men lifted the coffin to shoulder height. "With me gentlemen." The funeral director walked in front of them at a sedate pace into the crematorium, along the corridor and into the chapel. As they walked slowly down the central aisle, none of the lads looked at the congregation fearing that any sight of a loved one would break their concentration on keeping their emotions in check. They placed the coffin on the plinth and turned to face the assembled mourners. Sean joined his Mum and sister on the first pew. Jimmy, Symon and Sid sat behind them. The vicar stood up to the podium and began the service. A few psalms and hymns later, the vicar nodded to Sean who stood and slowly walked to the podium. "Firstly, thank you for coming and providing your support during this period. Such occasions are naturally sad affairs and so they should be but Dad was never one to dwell on the bad side of life, instead choosing to always be positive and present a confident outlook to his family. I like to think that this above all else has been passed on to my sister and I. It might seem strange to say such things about a man who ultimately saw no future and finally could see no positive aspect to his situation and so ended his life but in the days following his death I have come to believe the opposite. His last words to us, in the form of a letter, explained his state of mind. Though I will never agree that he was the cause for any problems that existed, I do agree that he was and always would be ... and perhaps only could be ... a farmer. He was brought up with the love of countryside and the smell of the soil in his blood. He always provided for his family be that emotionally, financially or spiritually. We may have to trust more or search harder to find that spiritual and emotional support from him but I have no doubt we will. We are at a period in our lives now where change was compulsory and that was a step too far for Dad. He had done all he felt he could and left us with the best legacy he was able." Sean, on the edge of tears and with a crack in his voice, turned to his Mum and sister before continuing, "I hope we all take the best of memories from his time with us and wish him green pastures wherever he tends his flock." Sean walked from the podium back to his Mum and sister and sat down as Jimmy, Symon and Sid, along with the majority of the men in the congregation fought back the tears. The vicar stood again and read another couple of easily forgettable psalms. They ended with the hymn Jerusalem as Sean and his family lead everyone out of the chapel. As Jimmy, Symon and Sid arrived at the exit of the crematorium, Sean was waiting for them. "Eats and drinks back at the farmhouse, k?" Jimmy shook his hand. "Beautiful speech mate. Beautiful." Symon and Sid gave him a quick hug and muttered further words of appreciation. Sean went back to his Mum and sister to shake the hands of the congregation as they left. First out were Jimmy's parents. His Dad stood looking awkward in black jeans and a black jumper while his Mum grabbed Sean and hugged him like she never wanted to let him go. As Jimmy's Dad dragged her away he mouthed to Jimmy "See you at the wake." Jimmy nodded. Next was Paul, much to Jimmy's surprise, arm-in-arm with his sister Vickie. Paul saw the shock in Jimmy's eyes and rather than have any kind of explanatory conversation with him at that time, also motioned to him that they would see him later at the farmhouse. Sid's parents came next and after greeting Sean came over to the lads and spoke briefly about the service before making their goodbyes and heading off to the farm. Others came and went and as Jimmy was about to suggest to the lads that they too head off for the wake, Steph and Ginny walked out of the crematorium and up to Sean. The two girls hugged Sean, his Mum and sister before coming over to Jimmy, Symon and Sid. Jimmy gave Steph a big hug and said "It's great that you came up to this." Steph smiled. "Well to be honest, Ginny gave us no choice." She motioned towards Ginny who was hugging Symon. An older couple walked up behind Steph and Ginny. "This is my mum and dad." Steph said, making the introductions. "Hello gents. I've heard a lot about you all. Way too much." Steph's dad said as she playfully punched his arm. "Can we give you a lift to the wake Symon?" her dad asked. "You can show us the way." Symon nodded. Steph hugged Jimmy and said "See you there." before walking with her parents, Ginny and Symon to the car park. Jimmy and Sid followed them at a distance and hopped into the car.

The farmyard was packed with cars and the house heaving with guests. Knowing the place very well, Jimmy and Sid grabbed a couple of beers and walked through to the back of the house and settled into the comfortable sofas that filled the shabby 'family room' that looked out across the sloping fields of the farm to the bustling M5 in the distance. Shortly afterwards, Symon arrived with Ginny on his arm and Steph in tow. They sat together with Jimmy and Sid and looked out onto the vista. "It was a lovely service I thought. I'm not one for religion but I though Sean's speech was beautiful. From the heart." Steph said to nobody in particular. Everyone nodded in silent agreement. They all sat quietly sipping their drinks for the next few minutes. "I wonder what's going to happen for Sean next? His father ... did what he did ... because the farm was broke." Jimmy asked. At that moment, Sean walked in. "Hi folks. Thanks for coming. I figured you'd all be here. I needed to get away from everyone shaking my hand and telling me that I'm the head of the family now! Like I don't already know!" Sean flopped into his favourite chair opposite the sofas. He pulled at his tie and opened his top button. "So what does come next mate?" Jimmy asked. "Well, every cloud has a silver lining. I sat down with mum and sis on Sunday night and we had a good chat about the future. We discussed selling the land and the farm and what we might individually do in the future. Mum didn't have a clue what she could do having been a farmer's wife all her life. Sis said all she knew were horses and was too big to become a jockey!" The assembled audience chuckled politely. "And me ... well I told them that recently I had been considering joining the army. I enjoyed being a cadet as a kid and to be honest it's the only thing I could think of outside of farming. It would keep me outdoors." Jimmy stuttered a "But ... you could get shot!" Sean laughed for the first time since they'd rushed back from Cornwall. "I've been hunting once with you and the same could be said for that mate!" Everyone felt the mood lighten and joined in with the laughter. "Well they wouldn't have it anyway. Mum and sis both said they couldn't risk losing me after losing dad, so that's a non starter. So I suggested that we think about a way by which we could all live together for the foreseeable future, keep the land and do something other than farming. Sis suggested that she had always wanted to start a horse riding school and that mum would be a great help in that. We could build some more stables, buy some more horses and tack and advertise. It could bring in some money and keep them happy so I was all for it." Sid spoke next. "Um, not wishing to be the devil's advocate here but where are you going to get the money for new stables, horses and stuff?" Sean smiled. "Well, we got in touch with the NFU who held dad's life insurance policy. To be honest I was only doing it to let them know that he wouldn't be paying any more premiums. They were amazing. They expressed their condolences and asked me to hold for a minute. Then they came back to me and said the cheque would be in the post, made out to mum and would be with us in a couple of days." Sid looked confused. "Cheque? For what?" Sean smiled. "Exactly my question to them. They paid out the policy in full. I wasn't exactly keen on arguing with them but felt I should reiterate that he had committed suicide and she said that didn't matter. He'd had the policy for twenty odd years so they paid out. Yesterday the cheque arrived. £375,000!" Sid stammered a few 'buts'. "I know! Hollywood got it wrong all this time! So anyway, we have the money to survive and put some plans into place for the future." Jimmy looked at Sean. "What about you? What plans for you?" Sean nodded. "Well it got me thinking. Perhaps it is possible to turn the things that made the farm untenable as a farm to our favour. We're on the edge of a major city that is growing daily. I love the outdoors and want to be outdoors as much as possible. We've got plenty of land, just not enough to farm viably. What do you reckon to me setting up a paintball company?" Jimmy, Sid, Symon, Steph and Ginny looked at each other before replying in a garbled conglomeration "Great idea! Excellent! Awesome!" and other such words of agreement and enthusiasm. "It means we can keep the land pretty much as is but develop a few copses and woods. We can live in the house and I can utilise my cadet and hunting experience. I thought about perhaps also doing some hunting training where they use paintball guns and hunt targets not live animals. Steph smiled. "For all the vegetarians all over the world I thank you, Sean." Sean leant back into his chair. "So that's me sorted. What about you lot?" He looked at Symon. Symon looked at Ginny and grinned. "Well I got some great news today actually. It seems that Ginny and Steph's dad is a scout and has some pull at Plymouth Argylle. He's spoken with the manager and got me a month's trial down there." Sean, Jimmy and Sid erupted with congratulations. "Awww that's excellent news mate. You'll do well down there I am sure. But we'll miss you." said Jimmy. "Well at least you know the way there now. Though if I do well I will probably be living nearer Newquay than Plymouth." he said as he winked at Ginny. "Just don't break your leg surfing!" Sid joked. "I promise. And I do have a good teacher." Ginny smiled. Sean looked at Sid next. "Well I've decided that perhaps BAe is not the worst thing I can do. There's a reason behind why my family has worked there for generations and it's not just that they don't like commuting long distances! It's a good company that pays well and it's a good life. So as soon as we got back from Newquay I put in my application. I've got an interview next week for an apprenticeship. If I get it I'll be on good money and a career path. I have no dreams of being anything spectacular. I just want a nice family life. I want a family and a happy wife. Big tits optional."

Everyone, even Steph and Ginny, laughed. "So, that leaves Jimmy." Sean said looking his way. Jimmy shrugged. "I've got to be honest, I've no set plans for the BIG future. I've loved working on the car and the satisfaction of completing it is something that will live with me always. I can't really get passionate about working for Paul. He's a great bloke and brilliant boss but ... well who gets excited about replacing glass?" Sid looked at Jimmy. "What about becoming a mechanic? You could work with cars all day then." Jimmy agreed. "Yeah I could do that and certainly it would be within my skill set now I think though obviously there is still plenty to learn. But again, it doesn't ..." Steph smiled at him. "Get the juices flowing?" Jimmy nodded. "So what does Jimmy? Forget working, forget common sense, forget career paths. What do you really enjoy?" Jimmy thought for a moment. "When I first started working for Paul I was a dum kid with no education to speak of and an accent broader than my dad's. In my time with him I have learned about history, geography, people, science, business and a myriad other things. He helped me believe that my brain was not the dead lump inside my head but an empty and woefully under-utilised receptacle that *could* if properly taught and given the chance be more than it had been or had ever considered being. So you ask what I want? I want to learn. I want to experience. Our trip down to Newquay was more than a drive, a few days with the lads, a chance meeting with some wonderful people," he looked at Steph and smiled, "it was everything and more. It was adventure. It was educational. It was real life but outside of the classroom." Sean looked seriously at Jimmy. "So ... where does that take you?" Jimmy became enthusiastic. "Exactly!" the gathered friends looked confused. Jimmy explained, "Where does it take me? I need to travel. I need to experience life outside of the small community that I have loved but only known. I need to get on a plane and find life and knowledge. So that's what I am going to do. I'm going to talk with Paul and I know he'll be supportive. I'm going to save up and just go travelling and see where life leads me." Symon smiled. "I think that's a brilliant idea. But you have to promise me one thing." Jimmy looked across. "What's that?" Symon continued, "If I ever get to play at Wembley, you drop everything and leave whatever hole you've landed in and come back to watch the game. Deal?" Jimmy laughed. "Of course. Anything for you mate." Symon offered his hand which Jimmy took and shook. "That's a promise that you'd better not break!" Jimmy looked seriously into Symons eyes and replied, "I promise." It was Sid's turn to speak. "Well I'm not exactly planning to play at Wembley but I want a similar BMD promise. If I get married or have a child or ultimately leave this planet, I want you there. Simple. Deal?" he held out his hand. Jimmy shook it and said, "Of course." Sean cleared his throat. "I was hoping that you might come in on this paintball thing with me cos I'll need a mechanic and strong hands but just as I have to try to do what I think will make me and mine happy, so must you. Mine is a reverse request promise. As we will no doubt all be present at the major events in each others lives," he said motioning to Symon and Sid, "so must you ensure we are able to be with you for **your** major events. You get married? We'd better get an invite with plenty of notice to arrange the stag do! You have a kid? We want to be there to wet the baby's head and argue over which one of us the baby is named after. Deal?" Jimmy stood up and walked over to Sean who stood up to meet him. He shook his hand and pulled him in for a hug which Symon and Sid jumped up and joined. Ginny and Steph looked at each other and jumped up to join in the mass scrum.

Bristle

Conclusion

In the weeks that followed, Jimmy talked with Paul and explained his plans. Paul could not have been more supportive while showing his reticence at his leaving. He organised lots of overtime for Jimmy to help him save up. Sean quickly set up his sister's riding school which if things continued as they started would be a great success. Sid and Jimmy went over every weekend and helped with the paintball setup and had a great time at the opening event which got some local newspaper coverage but was most memorable for including all their friends from Newquay who came up with Symon and a bunch of players from Plymouth Argylle in tow in a luxury coach that struggled down the winding farm track but managed it. Sid got his apprenticeship with BAe and before long put down a deposit on a house and moved in with his nurse girlfriend. Symon managed to do well with the Plymouth under 21's and had played a couple of times for the first team. His agent had informed him that a couple of bigger clubs were interested in signing him but he had refused them believing that the best place for him until he fully proved himself was with Plymouth. I'm sure living near Ginny and the wonderful surfing of Newquay played no part in his decision. Jimmy had sold the car and at the paintball party had tried to give their share to Sean, Symon and Sid. They each told him to keep it as their contribution to his further education.

Jimmy had said his goodbyes to his parents when he left the house. Now he stood on the platform at Temple Meads station with a rucksack full to bursting, a heart full of trepidation and a mind expectant of experiences. Symon was in Plymouth but had texted him 'Good luck!' Sean and Sid had said their goodbyes the previous night. Only Paul and Vickie stood with him at the station. As the trained pulled in, Vickie hugged him tightly and with tears in her eyes told him to stay safe but enjoy himself. Paul waited his turn then shook his hand and gave him a big hug. "I've got your bonus here. I had a really good quarter and you deserve your share." He handed Jimmy an envelope which had written, in beautiful cursive writing, 'First round's on me." Jimmy tucked it into his front jeans pocket and thanked him. He hefted his rucksack onto his shoulders and boarded the train. Paul and Vickie followed him along the train until he found a compartment and settled into his seat up against the glass. As the train slowly pulled out, Paul and Vickie walked with it waving to him until the train sped out of the station and on towards London.

Made in the USA
Charleston, SC
28 November 2015